HAPPILY EVER CHRISTMAS

LAKESHIA POOLE

Jack of All Trades Media

P.O. Box 307

Sandersville, GA 31082

hello@jackofalltradesmedia.com

Happily Ever Christmas/ Lakeshia Poole -- 1st ed.

Another Happy Christmas story for Betty :)

CHAPTER ONE

"*M*erry Christmas to you too."
I didn't mean it. But I had to say it to get my client off the phone.

You have to repeat the phrase all of December. Otherwise, people would swear you were a heartless Scrooge.

"That was the driest Merry Christmas I ever heard," my coworker Samantha said, pointing her pen at me. "You sounded like a kid who didn't get anything she wanted under the tree."

"We don't have time for all the pleasantries." I ran my fingers down the bone-straight ends of my hair. I was still getting used to the silky tresses instead of my thick, tight curls. My hairstylist called it the Anna Wintour bob and said the style made me look like a boss. *Whatever.*

I rarely straightened my hair, and I missed twirling the ends when I got stressed.

"I didn't think they'd ever stop talking about their Christmas plans, and let us actually get to work."

My laptop dinged, alerting me that only 15% of the

battery remained. That's about how much energy I felt like I had left.

What was supposed to be a 30-minute call recapping the product launch event for our client, Thin Quick, had turned into a two-hour brainstorm.

Samantha and I huddled in the comfy crème leather chairs in the sitting area of my office. Sunlight poured in through the floor-to-ceiling windows shining a natural spotlight on the yellow sticky notes and stacks of file folders covering the round table between us.

I promise there was a method to our messy madness. Corporations like Thin Quick turned to our public relations firm to bring their products and brands to life and to the masses. The fancy word we used to sell these services was experiential marketing. But it all boiled down to coordinating large-scale events that attracted a lot of attention, positive press, and sales.

"Well, at least the Thin Quick people are happy," Samantha said. "It's not every day you hear praise like that from your largest client."

"They're so pleased, they gave us extra work. *Yay.*"

With everyone resolving to lose a few pounds, December and January were the biggest sales periods for Thin Quick. After a successful Los Angeles event and PR launch, they wanted us to replicate the same type of campaign in New York—in less than a month.

"But, extra work means we can ask for extra budget." Samantha rubbed invisible money between her fingertips, raising an eyebrow.

"And around here, extra budget makes everybody happy," I laughed.

More funds to close out the year would certainly make

our firm's Managing Director Paula *extra* happy. Paula had all but promised to bump me up to my dream title of Vice President if I continued to bring in new business. Expanding the Thin Quick account by another $100K would earn me the promotion I deserved.

Finally, all of the 14-hour days, restless nights, traveling last minute from city-to-city would pay off!

"Make sure you send the final report from the launch event to Paula too. Include all the social media analytics too — she'll love the fact that the Thin Quick shake was the #1 trending topic. I'll update her on the new proposal and budget."

I typed and talked fast, chomping off half a cinnamon-raisin bagel. Even though it approached 2:30 pm, I hadn't finished breakfast yet. Bitter and black coffee wasn't ideal at room temperature, but I gulped down the much-needed caffeine anyway.

Samantha ticked off all of the ideas the client had thrown out during our call. A lot of them weren't viable on such a short timeline in the midst of the holidays, but we always aimed to make it happen.

We were halfway through brainstorming alternative ideas for the new proposal when my laptop's screen went black.

Oh, shoot! I knew better, but I pressed the power button repeatedly, hoping it would come back on.

"If we do something like 'New Year in New York,' we can get a celebrity party host and serve the shakes in little shot glasses. Or maybe a celebrity trainer would be better?" Samantha asked.

As I was about to answer, the phone rang, lighting up red.

3

I picked up on the second ring. "This is Ebony."

"It's Kim. I have your sister Alexis on line 1. She says it's an emergency."

I could only imagine what my drama queen sister-*in-law* Alexis wanted. Something was always going on with my older brother Manny and his wife.

Nine-times out of 10, their problem was financial. I'd set up a special checking account for them to keep these 'emergency calls' to a minimum.

"Tell her I'll call her back after my meeting." I pressed the speakerphone button OFF to return to my discussion with Samantha.

"Where was I? I like the idea of a host, but I don't think a trainer will get us the attention we want."

"I guess it is the same as what everybody else does."

"Right. And we don't want people to think of Thin Quick as the usual 'diet.' It's a lifestyle brand."

The muted television I kept on to stay on the pulse of breaking news caught my attention. The gorgeous singer Lourdés Michele threw her head back in laughter. She looked like a modern-day Marilyn Monroe but with fire-red hair instead of blond.

Known more for her provocative selfies, swimsuit photoshoots, and Hollywood romances than hit songs, Lourdés was the 'it' celebrity of the moment.

"I want to make her the new face of Thin Quick."

Samantha twisted in her chair to get a good look at the screen. "Okay. She is definitely something different."

"We may have to prep her for media interviews, but she loves the camera. And it loves her right back. Usually, TV makes you look bigger, but she is perfect on-screen," I said.

"She's almost too good to be true." Samantha's chair

squished as she shifted, crossing her legs. "I can see why Thin Quick would want her as a spokesperson. I think their customers wish they had a body like hers, but does this approach feel a little too perfect?"

"There's no such thing as too perfect. We have to sell people on what they think they want. Even if it's a little unrealistic."

"I know I'd buy a truckload of Thin Quick meals if I believed they could make me look like Lourdés," Samantha muttered.

"Exactly! So, if you could work with legal to draft a contract that we can send over for the client to review along with the proposal, that'll help keep everything moving."

I walked over to my desktop computer. It chimed at the arrival of a new message at the same time my cell phone buzzed.

Alexis' number and picture popped up on the screen—it was a photo of her playing air guitar in front of the Elvis statue in Memphis. I tapped IGNORE to silence the call and pulled up my e-mail inbox.

Click.

Scroll.

Delete.

Happy Holidays and out-of-office e-mails crowded out important messages from clients and staff. I wished I could automatically send the end of year notes to the trash. Scratch that, I wished I could toss the whole of December and return to business as usual.

I clicked through the Thin Quick files until I found a collage of images, showcasing before and after pictures of real Thin Quick customers. Short, tall. Pear-shaped. Narrow as a 2x4 beam. A cross-section of ethnicities and ages. All of these women had stories, either wanting to lose or gain a few pounds. Some battled weight challenges since childhood, and others faced health crises that nearly stole their lives. They overcame incredible odds, not to be skinny, but to be healthier and happier.

I attached the photos and testimonies that tugged at the heart to a new e-mail message for Samantha. "I'm sending you some photos and customer reviews I want featured on the campaign website."

Samantha scooted to the edge of the chair, laptop wobbling on her knees.

"We discussed quite a lot today. The new proposal, contracts, and I'll have to do some research for our budget. You want the website updated today too?"

My eyes glued to the computer monitor, I flashed a smile. "That would be perfect!"

"I was hoping to leave a little early, so I could make the office Christmas party." Her voice was as strained as the smile plastered on her face.

Having worked with Samantha for over six years, I noticed she did this thing when she didn't agree with someone, stretching out the end of words into a sing-song. It reminded me of how moms talked to their children when they refused to share or take turns on the playground slide.

"If you've been to one office Christmas party, haven't you been to them all?" I asked, shrugging.

"Well, I won't be able to stay long because I have to catch a flight home for the holidays."

"You're taking off this early?" I paused to look at the calendar, counting the time left before Christmas with the oval tip of my nude-colored pinky nail – 12 days.

"I'll work from home for a few days," Samantha said.

"My entire family is in California. It's the only time of year we're together, so it's a whole thing."

"I get that Christmas is a big deal, but that leaves us with only a couple weeks to nail down logistics."

I said I understood the hype around Christmas, but it didn't make sense to take off half the month of December for one holiday.

Do you really need that much vacation time?

There was a part of me that liked having the office to myself. I was way more productive without the noise, banter about the weekend, interruptions, and distractions of other people.

Last year, I nibbled on leftover holiday client gifts— Harry and David sweets, an Edible Arrangements fruit bouquet, good cheese, and roasted Virginia peanuts. I hosted a cocktail party of one. And the work got done. That's all I asked of Samantha, that we complete our work with excellence.

"We'll just use all the same documents and plans from the L.A. event as templates. Have the intern do the initial research. And you should be able to knock out these website changes quickly. Besides, they still have wi-fi on planes, right?" I asked with a chuckle. "You can get a lot done on a long flight."

"Of course." Samantha forced a smile so tight and wide, it had to hurt. "Oh, before I forget. Here's your gift. Merry Christmas."

She dropped it in a thud on my desk. I imagined it was a fruit-scented candle or maybe another mug with some inspirational saying scrawled across the front. The gift bag matched Samantha's atrocious sweater dress. Wooly and bright red, it featured every Christmas symbol imaginable. Santa's jolly, pink-cheeked face. Candy canes and gingerbread men. Golden lights ringed around her curvy frame. I believe I spotted the three wise men walking on her shoulder.

Samantha's get-up was part of the office's "Ugly Christmas Sweater Party." I had thrown on my usual costume of black pants, white button-down, and a gray cardigan. I planned to opt-out of all the 'fun' to meet Thin Quick's deadlines.

"Thanks for this." I made a mental note to ship out a card and gift to her, because she surely wasn't on my gift list. Truth be told I didn't even have a list.

"Do you need anything else before I'm out of the office?"

"I think that will be all. If I need anything, I'll send you a quick e-mail."

"Ebony, I'm not checking e-mail over Christmas. Everybody will be out of the office, including our client."

Was that a dig at the fact that I would likely be the only person toiling away with budget worksheets and tinkering with venue layouts instead of sipping eggnog and unwrapping gifts?

Before I could react, our receptionist Kim poked her head in.

"I'm so sorry to interrupt your meeting, but it's your sister. Again. She threatened to," Kim paused to look at the note she'd written, pushing her glasses to the tip of her nose. "In her words, 'come up here and get you her-doggone-self,' if I didn't put her through."

Like I said, drama queen.

"Sure, send the call through," I sighed, holding a finger up to Samantha. "This should only take a moment."

I picked up the phone before it finished the first ring.

"Alexis, what in the world is —"

"Manny's in the hospital." She dropped the news in a breathless cry. "He's in the emergency room right now. The ambulance came and picked him up. One minute he was up on the ladder, then the next—"

"Wait, what? Slow down." I rose and turned my back to Samantha, feeling more in control of the situation standing up. Besides, I didn't want anybody seeing the breakdown I felt coming on.

"...I don't know...maybe a heart attack, but I've been at the hospital for over an hour now, and they won't tell me nothing..."

Walls bearing framed pictures of client events across the world closed in on me. Normally, the expansive view of downtown Atlanta stirred a sense of bold confidence within, but now I felt light-headed. Like I was falling. Dark gray clouds gathered over the city. Over me. The sparkling clean glass reflected the visage of a fearful girl instead of my face. Coldness emanated from the thick window, but all I felt was heat, burning from my toes up.

Worry I hadn't met in a long time filled my eyes. I pressed the silver cross necklace against my lips, a wordless prayer ran through my mind. I wanted to yell for Alexis to stop talking, but I knew what this was like. I'd been here before.

"...I can't go through this by myself. You need to come home, Ebony. Just in case..."

My sister-in-law's frantic cries sounded eerily like the voices I'd heard deliver the worst news of my life 10 years ago. Alexis became a muffled sound far away, the steady pounding of my heart filling my ears.

A heart attack at his age? My brother isn't even 40 years old yet. God, this isn't fair.

As if it would hold me together, I hugged my chest, the silver and gold charms on my bracelet jingling. I couldn't stop shaking.

"Hey, is everything okay?" Samantha eked out, startling me from both past and present tragedies.

Warm tears streamed down my cheeks. I closed my eyes, not wanting to see that girl anymore. I wished I could shut out everybody and everything, especially the dire news about my brother.

"I have to go home."

CHAPTER TWO

When I left Aurbor Grove 10 years ago, I swore I'd never return. I didn't want to revisit the tragic night that changed my life. I definitely didn't want to deal with the judgmental stares and whispers behind my back about what I did.

So far, I'd been able to keep that promise and create the perfect, new life. I worked very hard, being the best and giving my best so that I could get the best. When I was a little girl, dreaming up my future, my plan didn't look exactly like this, but I was close enough.

One sentence made me want to risk it all: "Manny's in the hospital."

My brother was all I had left in this world. The thought of life without him put everything in focus — all that other stuff became a blurry background, second tier, and meaningless in a minute. And I felt foolish for ever seeing it all differently.

The last time I saw Manny was six months ago. After plotting and planning for months, we found a date that worked with my hectic schedule. We met in Atlanta, catching up over cheese dip and crispy fried chicken tacos at my favorite lunch spot, Taqueria del Sol. For hours, we talked about everything from the Atlanta Falcons to the financial crisis.

Manny had grand plans—for his family and the business. He excitedly shared bold, audacious ideas about transforming the Aurbor Grove Inn into a destination for vacations, weddings, and special occasions. He wanted to take the small bed and breakfast our parents established to the next level. And based on the level of passion in his voice, I believed he would.

I remember thinking how proud they would be of him for carrying on their vision, then selfishly wondering what they'd think of me for abandoning it.

What if that was the last time I saw him?

I closed my eyes, inhaled deeply. Searching. Flipping through the memories of that day. The smile that stretched wide when he first saw me made me feel warm on the inside. But I couldn't remember what he wore or the sound of his voice.

Did I tell him I loved him?

I wanted to run out of the office, but I could not move. My personal, private life crashed head-on into my professional one, rendering me paralyzed.

"Ebony? Ebony, you're scaring me." Samantha's voice cut through the haze of emotions, thoughts, and memories.

"I-I have to go home." A quiet urgency filled my tone, but my pumps were rooted to the carpet.

Samantha gently took the phone from my hand, the dial tone blaring. "What happened? What's wrong?" she asked.

"My brother's in the hospital. He may have had a heart attack, or something? I don't know. My sister...she was hysterical. I have to go, now."

I stumbled toward my desk, gripping the edge. Taking a deep breath, I willed myself to get it together. I wanted, no, I needed to be strong – for myself, Manny, and Alexis. But that girl in the glass haunted me.

"Sit down for a moment."

Samantha guided me to my chair, her hands on my shoulders. She offered to take me home. And she wasn't talking about my condo down the street. She was willing to shift her plans to drive me *home-home* three hours away to Aurbor Grove.

She knew that I didn't drive. Technically, I could but chose not to get behind the wheel. Sometimes that was tough in a city like Atlanta, but I managed. Living downtown made it easier – everything I needed was a few blocks or a train stop away. Anyplace farther outside the perimeter, I relied on UBER or Lyft. Getting from Atlanta to Aurbor Grove during rush hour would prove to be trickier.

I sunk in my chair, staring out at the bumper-to-bumper traffic building on Peachtree Street. Beads of rain slid down the window, surely doubling commute times.

I need to go home.

The bright white Ferris wheel near Centennial Park turned slowly. Manny loved stuff like that—whether climbing to the tallest branch on a tree or hopping on the craziest ride at the amusement park. He always had to drag me along on his adventures.

"Give me your cell. I'll call your sister to let her know I'm bringing you home," Samantha said. I didn't fight it – the usual rebel inside gave up quite easily.

"Hi, yes, this is actually Ebony's coworker, Samantha..." she began, stepping a few feet away. A few minutes later, she handed my phone back to me.

"Alexis said she told you that she had sent someone to

pick you up. Maybe you missed that part. I know it's a lot to take in." Samantha made a pained expression of pity, tucking a blond strand behind her studded ear. She had that mom voice on again, but it was warm and tender, and I needed that right now.

"I made sure she had the correct address, and I'll tell the security desk to send them straight up." Samantha glanced at her neon pink watch that also calculated every step and wink of sleep. "Your sister said your ride should arrive in a couple of hours, but I can wait with you. I don't mind skipping the party."

"No, no," I sniffled, waving her away. "You need to go. I will be fine. And I'm sure my brother will be fine too."

At least I hope so, I thought as Samantha hugged me goodbye.

* * *

As ALWAYS, my boss Paula was last to leave the office.

She emphasized that as head of the firm—she was first in and last to leave. Having given the staff an early release for the Christmas party, she too departed much earlier.

"I feel so bad leaving you here alone." She balanced her purse and gift bags in her arms. Her sweater wasn't nearly as ugly as Samantha's. Dancing reindeer raised up their hooves over the words: Ready to Party.

"I promise I will be okay."

I hadn't cried in an hour. Crunching the numbers for a tight budget kept my mind so occupied, I didn't think about my brother lying in a hospital bed.

"I was able to catch up on the Thin Quick account," Paula said.

That sent my anxiety antenna straight up.

"The L.A. launch event drew our largest crowds and some of the best media coverage ever," she said. "The client sounds extremely satisfied. And it's certainly nice for us to get some extra budget before year-end."

"I couldn't have done it without Samantha and the rest of the team."

"Thanks to your leadership," she said. "Well, I have some gifts for you." She placed a shimmery, gold bag and another file atop all the others on my desk. The shiny, red Christmas bow stuck on the manila folder caught the glint of the fluorescent light hovering overhead.

Opening the folder to the offer letter for Vice President, my eyes widened. It outlined my new job description, duties, and management responsibilities.

Talk about a bittersweet day.

"It's not official until you sign off on the paperwork," she began, her voice dropping to a whisper, "and I hope you will."

My mouth hung open a little when my eyes ran across the salary increase, perks, and bonus. This job would push me into a new tax bracket.

I started spending the money – in my mind – immediately. I could upgrade my kitchen, get those shoes I'd been eyeing, take a real vacation...

"I want you to take the lead on all major corporate accounts for our Atlanta, New York, and D.C. offices."

"Oh my God," I muttered.

Have you ever wanted something so badly, that when you finally got it, you just didn't know how to act? I wanted to leap into her arms, but I clasped my hands together and held them against my lips.

"I cannot thank you enough."

"Don't thank me. You have given your very best on every

single project," Paula said. "You'll have to hit the ground running, so get plenty of rest over the holidays. Take care of yourself and your family."

"We still have some things to—"

"Uh-uh. You're off the next week." She shook her head and wagged a finger. "Today's your last day until *after* Christmas."

"I usually don't take Christmas off. Really, I don't mind working," I said.

"Ebony, when you move to this level, you have to know how to delegate. Your team can't grow if you don't give them the opportunity to take on more responsibilities."

"But, what if something goes wrong?"

Paula tossed her head back, laughing. "It probably will. Isn't Samantha your Account Director? Let her put out the fires. She has to learn how to run the account without you."

"Wait, you're taking the Thin Quick account away from me?"

"No, it will still be your account. But so will a dozen others, so managing your time is key," Paula said. "As a VP your job won't be to manage the day-to-day details, but people. You will still be the client's main point of contact, but you won't have to worry about the weeds anymore. Just maintain the forest."

But what if I liked the weeds? While excited about the promotion, it felt like Paula was ripping my baby from my arms. All I could think of were the worst-case scenarios happening on the Thin Quick account, and I wouldn't be there to fix things. Sure, I had capable colleagues, but sometimes they didn't do things the right way — my way.

Then it dawned on me, I'd never managed teams across multiple offices. I was moving up faster than most at my age.

And the way Paula described the new role, it would be a huge transition from what I was most familiar with doing.

What if I wasn't ready for that level of management?

"Give Samantha the reins on Thin Quick," Paula interrupted the internal mini-meltdown.

"No," I almost shouted. "I mean, I don't know if that's a good idea. She's traveling home today, and I'd hate to drop everything on her."

"I'm sure she can manage from home. Isn't it pretty much the same tasks from the L.A. event? I'll also reach out to the New York office to get a team together that can help out too."

"But — "

"Let them take care of it. I'm serious. I better not get any e-mails from you. Not one. I need you fresh. Can you do that for me?" she asked, but didn't wait for an answer.

Once the frosted glass doors to our office suite closed behind Paula, I picked up my phone to call Manny and tell him my good news. His cell phone went straight to voicemail and when I heard his voice asking me to leave a message, I remembered where he was.

What if I never heard that voice again?

Nobody counseled or celebrated with me like my big brother. I could not imagine my life without Manny.

"God, please help me get through this," I whispered.

That was as much of a prayer I could bring myself to say. Truthfully, anger surged on the inside. None of this made sense to me. Our family had already gone through so much loss and pain, now my brother. There's only so much bending you can do before you break, right?

I dialed Manny's number just to hear him again.

* * *

THE STORM WAS LONG GONE, and the city buildings at my back lit up as the sun drifted lower. By the time the sky went from fuchsia and orange watercolors to inky black, I'd finished the New York event proposal and started sketching out content ideas for the campaign website.

Since Paula wouldn't allow me to touch my account until after Christmas, I wanted to get as much done as possible.

The TV on full volume, a reporter warned that traffic was worse than usual because of the earlier surprise rain showers.

I wondered if whoever was coming to pick me up would get delayed. In the mix of emotions, I didn't think to ask Samantha for a name when she called Alexis to check on my ride.

Oh God, I hope it's not my cousin Gwen. She's going to talk me to death about people and places I don't know. But there was no way Gwen would volunteer to fight through Atlanta traffic. She refused to drive an hour outside of town.

I thumbed in a quick message to Alexis, asking about my ride.

The ellipsis letting me know that she was typing a response popped up on the phone screen, then disappeared. A few seconds later, the three dots within a conversation bubble appeared again.

Finally, her message came through.

Alexis: He will be there soon.

It shouldn't have taken her that long to tap out such a short answer. And it still didn't answer my question.

"But who is he?" I said aloud as I typed.

The dots played hide-and-go-seek on my screen alerting me that once again she was starting and stopping a message.

It took her just as long to type an even shorter message this time.

One name.

My eyes bugged out, and the phone tumbled onto the carpet.

CHAPTER THREE

"Jackson? You've got to be kidding me. Not him."

Now you might have said there were millions of "Jackson"s in the world, and I shouldn't panic. That I should probably calm down and back away from the sweet snacks I raided from the kitchen.

Too late. Downing the sugary mix of caramel-coated popcorn, chocolate-covered peanuts, and a Cherry Coke lifted my spirit, energy level, and heart rate.

Maybe "Jackson" was a professional driver or a neighbor? But I knew my family. They didn't have that kind of money. And there was only one Jackson that should *not* pick me up, and based on Alexis' hemming and hawing over text messages, it was likely that one.

The one who'd held my hand on half a dozen first days of school, at college orientation, and promised to hold it through anything.

Until I let go.

Our years together – being silly kids on the playground, hanging out at each other's houses, plotting our perfect paths under the stars, him on bended knee, me crying on his shoulder – flashed across the screen of my mind like a slideshow of snapshots from a life long-forgotten.

What we had shared felt too simple to classify as love. That girl was so naïve, and that guy too carefree. They would have done anything for each other, but when reality hit, neither could overcome it.

That was a sign it wasn't meant to be, right? If we couldn't handle that storm, we surely couldn't weather a lifetime together?

Why my sister-in-law thought it would be a good idea to send my ex-fiancé to bring me home, I had no clue. Drama, drama, drama.

Of all the people! Now, I know Aurbor Grove was a small town, but it wasn't *that* small.

The swoop sound notifying me of the arrival of another text message sounded extra loud in the deserted office.

Alexis: Manny told him to.

She knew I couldn't get upset if it were Manny's wish. After all, it was Manny who'd convinced Jackson to ask me out in the first place. Jackson approached me in the school cafeteria, all nervous and stammering. Then he blurted out, "Manny told me to."

This guy, the sickest he's ever been, never ceased to amaze me. From the hospital bed, he sent the guy I'd least expect or want to rescue me.

I figured Jackson wasn't thrilled about the trip either, but I guess Manny thought this was one chance to get us together again. Either it would be a happy reunion or entertaining story to add to his collection.

Imagining his howling laughter brought a smile to my face. Then a soft laugh of my own. Happy and sad tears mixed with snot bubbles followed. All that hysteria burst open to the cheerful soundtrack of Mariah Carey belting "Santa Claus is Comin' to Town" on a TV commercial.

"You better watch out, you better not cry..."

"You are singing the truth, Mariah," I chuckled to myself, bopping in my seat.

Oh yeah, the sugar was working its magic.

"Hey...Ebony." I jumped at Jackson's deep voice laced with a Southern twang.

My eyes traveled up from a pair of polished boots to Jackson's broad shoulders and finally, his face. He had the same dreamy hazel eyes I used to get lost in. A thick beard framed the lips that'd been my first kiss. His 6'2" frame touched the crinkled silver, ribbons flowing from the mini-wreath hanging over my doorway.

I think I said hello back, but it was so soft I didn't even hear myself.

Jackson cleared his throat, then called out my name again. "You ready?"

"Uhhh, yeah."

No, I'm not, I thought. I assumed with all the time that'd passed between us, I'd be ready to see him again. That I'd built a wall around my heart, thick and strong enough to withstand his presence. One look and a few words, and I was a dopey teenager again.

"Yeah, I...let me get my things." I shuffled through files and stuffed them in my bag.

The last time I saw Jackson I was pressing the ring he'd given to me back into his palm. He wouldn't let go of my hand and refused to accept my decision to leave him and Aurbor Grove.

Over the years, I'd envisioned how our reunion would play out. Would he curse me or caress my cheek in forgiveness? He did neither – keeping a safe distance and disconcerting look in his eyes. I wondered if being this close made his heart tap-dance too.

"I see you're as organized as you've always been," he said.

"And you are as judgmental about it as you've always been."

His eyes darted from my desk to the industry awards and pictures of me with celebrities propped on the credenza, then rested on the framed degrees from Emory University.

Each carefully selected piece told of my life after Aurbor Grove, after us. I wondered what he thought of it all—of me. My accolades impressed most, but he seemed bored by it all. The petty side of me wanted to shout, 'Look at what I did without you and everybody else that doubted me!'

Sensing my struggle to get it together, Jackson rushed towards me. "Let me help you."

His hand brushed against mine as he reached for my laptop bag. He was so close that the whiff of his cologne made my stomach flip.

"It's good to see you," I admitted.

He flashed an awkward smile and offered a half-hug. When I didn't let go, he brought his other arm around. I wanted to be strong, but it felt good to be in Jackson's arms again. I surrendered, leaning into his warm embrace.

"Everything's going to be okay," he said softly, his lips grazing my ear.

I nodded my head against his chest, and he held me tighter.

I was safe with him. That's something I always knew for sure.

"Thank you for coming."

"Manny told me to," he whispered.

CHAPTER FOUR

jazzy version of "I'll Be Home for Christmas" filled the elevator, but quietness hovered between me and Jackson. I smoothed down the side of my bob, then the blunt-cut bangs. Our somberness was even visible in the blurry reflections on the silver doors.

I was going home alright, but I didn't know what state I'd find my brother in. On one hand, I worried, but on the other, I selfishly cursed Manny for causing this unexpected homecoming.

I could see the people now, hands over their mouths as they gossiped about my return. Surely, they'd bring up what happened because people never forget your worst episodes. They'll work your faults into the most innocent conversation.

'How are you doing since whatchamacallit did so-and-so?' they'd say. Or ask questions they knew the answers to just to get a reaction.

Counting down 15 floors and crossing the marble lobby lit up with gaudy Christmas decorations, Jackson only offered a line of a smile and nod to the officer at the U-shaped security desk.

He balanced my bags and holding the front door open for me.

"I talked to Alexis before I got here. She said they're still waiting on some results from a few tests. But otherwise, Manny's sleeping and doing better."

"Oh, thank God." I covered my heart with my palm. "I was so scared to call. I want to know, but then again, I don't want to know. I've been thinking the worst. And I don't think I can handle any more bad news."

"I know it's scary, but he was talking fine when I left him. Everything seemed okay, but we have to make sure."

I still had so many questions — mostly about Manny and a few about him. Like, what was he doing now? Was he in a relationship? Did he have kids? Despite their close friendship, Manny rarely brought up any Jackson updates. I always assumed he thought that was the safest thing to do — keep us separate. And then he pulled this stunt.

"I'm parked over there," he said, pointing his key fob. A chirp and flicker of yellow lights drew my attention to a truck backed crookedly in the visitor's parking space. The click-clack of my heels slowed to an off-beat clunk — the country had come to the city!

Stripes of red mud caked around the high tires and bed of Jackson's white Dodge Ram. I was sure I'd find fishing poles and a toolbox on the back of the truck.

He placed my bags in the back seat and had to help me get in the passenger side. I jumped when the Hemi engine roared to life in the empty parking deck. He turned down the smooth voice crooning about chestnuts roasting on an open fire streaming from the speakers and upped the heat.

"I figured you hadn't eaten anything, so I got you something."

I grabbed the plastic bag sitting on the center console, then unwrapped the turkey BLT sandwich and chips.

"That Cherry Coke is for you too," he said, nodding at the cupholder. "Is this okay? I wasn't sure about what you still liked."

"No, this is good."

"I mean, it's been so long, you could be vegetarian for all I know."

It has been a while, I thought, taking a bite.

I was thankful for the meal because my sugar high had worn off, leaving me extra hungry. And packing my mouth with food meant I didn't have to talk too much.

Jackson switched from the Christmas music to a sports talk show. Still silent, he only grunted at the stop-and-go traffic on I-75.

Once the lanes opened up, Jackson drove the speed limit, cars swooshing alongside and around him. "I don't see how you deal with that every day."

I balled up the empty wrapper and sipped some of the Cherry Coke.

"I don't drive anymore."

His eyes ran over me, a pained expression clouding his demeanor. He automatically knew why.

"It works out though," I said. "I know people who commute more than an hour each way."

"That's crazy."

Full and satisfied, I gathered the courage to ask about the details around Manny.

"What happened? Were you there?"

"So, Alexis was at a doctor's appointment. I was at the Inn, helping Manny put up decorations. You know he goes all out." Jackson paused to laugh. "In addition to all the lights and props, your brother insisted on adding Santa and his reindeer on the rooftop."

"Oh, God. He's always doing the most!" I chuckled.

"The Jingle Bell Festival is coming up, and all the businesses have a competition for best decorations. He has to win first place again."

"That sounds like my brother alright."

"You know how competitive he is."

"Yep."

"He was up on the ladder and said he felt funny. Then he reached for his chest. I asked if I need to come up and help him down."

As he recounted, Jackson glanced at me, each time lingering longer than the moment before.

"He told me he was alright and could make it down himself. I saw him grab his phone so I figured everything was good. Next thing I know, he somehow fell, and I called the ambulance."

I gasped, bringing my hands to my mouth. My nerves bounced all over the place, the warm tingling sensation flared up and down my body. I reminded myself that he was okay, but my imagination kept me stuck on the picture of him falling.

"What did the EMTs say?"

"They couldn't say if it was a heart attack or what. Like I said, he seems alright. I would've gone to the hospital with them, but Manny made me promise to come get you right then and there."

"Oh, Manny. Of all the things to worry about at that moment, he was thinking about me?"

"He knows how tough it can be for you," he said, clenching the steering wheel. "This time of year."

This time of year.

I leaned against the window, the thoughts and emotions about this time of year bubbling up. That young girl appeared in the glass again, reflecting against the blur of pine trees. A thinner, doe-eyed version of me going from excitement to excruciating pain.

This time of year.

The thing is I wanted to be happy so bad, but I could never muster up enough joy to fill the void. I didn't want to bring everybody else down, so I never mentioned it. I faked along, knowing that while the holidays boosted the spirits of others, they only made me think of what I lost. What I did. Guilt gnawed at me and the aching sadness that came every December overshadowed the Christmas cheer of this time of year.

That one night changed everything. Me. Manny. And it most definitely changed my relationship with Jackson.

To think of potentially losing my brother during the same time of year as well? It was too much to bear alone.

Glimpsing Jackson's profile, the moonlight cast a glow outlining the ridge of his nose and square jaw. Despite the long separation, his mere presence still brought an automatic sense of security. He fully understood the roller coaster of emotions looping within me, because he'd been there for me then and now.

I had a feeling Manny wasn't the sole reason Jackson came to get me.

"I wanted to come get you." He confessed, reading my mind like he used to do when we were younger. We always joked that the deep connection of finishing each other's thoughts and sentences was our magic trick.

"I thought you should be home," he said. His voice dropped lower. "I've missed you."

Despite the darkness surrounding and filling the truck, I felt him glancing at me, searching. Our eyes met, and the flitter in my belly soared into my chest.

I reached over and clasped his hand, squeezing tightly. His declaration made it easier for me to profess my own truth.

"I've missed you too."

CHAPTER FIVE

"*E*bony, wake up. We're here."

Jackson's husky voice jolted me awake. Wild-eyed and confused, I must've looked crazy because he quickly cupped my cheek. As he caressed my skin tenderly, those golden-brown eyes lulled me into a sweet calmness instantly.

"Hey, it's okay. I'm with you."

Funny enough, he'd been in my dreams too, but we'd reunited under random, but happier circumstances: an airplane ride. I'd dreamt we both ended up on the same flight, same row, and spent the whole trip laughing and talking. Before the real-life Jackson yanked me back to reality, I was inches away from kissing him in my dreams. The spike of heat and fluttering in my gut lingered.

Opening my eyes to see his dimpled half-smile made me want to return to the dream version of my life instead of this.

How did this man still have such power over me? It was unnerving.

I shook off the thoughts of what could be and dancing nerves, batting his hand away from my face.

"I'm fine."

"Okay, then. I was just..." Jackson let go of a deep sigh, and averted his eyes.

This was difficult for him too, and I knew my cold, curt responses only made it harder. But I needed to keep us both from making a reckless move based purely on emotion.

I was here for my brother — nothing more, nothing less. Jackson was simply my ride home.

"Visiting hours are over," he said, unbuckling his seatbelt. "But I know the nurse at the front desk, so I'm going to see if we can sneak in."

I remained in the warmth of Jackson's truck idling in the turnaround at the main entrance of Memorial Hospital. Tapping my fingers against the center console, I wasn't sure if I could handle seeing Manny in a hospital bed.

Hours away, I couldn't wait to get to him. Now that I was here, my nerves bounced all over the place, and in my mind's eye, I pictured him in the worst possible state.

The sliding glass doors rumbled open as Jackson walked to the front desk. Leaning his head and smiling wide, he sweet-talked the shapely woman standing in front of the counter.

I wasn't jealous or anything, but the way "Nurse Betty" played with his beard seemed a bit unprofessional if you asked me.

How well did he know her?

Maybe things had changed more than I thought. The last time I was at Memorial Hospital everything was snatched from me.

The exterior of the hospital had the same beige bricks

and aqua green signs surrounded by bushes. Two guys in matching khaki-colored scrubs smoked under the courtyard's gazebo decorated with twinkling red and green lights. An ambulance sat in front of the Emergency Room, its pulsing white and red lights extra bright against the pitch-black sky.

All of it whooshed me back to a decade before, and a heaviness rose within me.

"Get it together," I whispered, pushing it all back down. Jackson approached the truck, a twinkle of victory in his eyes. "We're good to go for a few hours," he said, hopping in the truck. He whipped it around and pulled into the nearly empty parking lot, quickly finding a space.

"I'm glad your friend could help. She seems nice."

He didn't react, and I bit my tongue to keep from asking more about her.

"You alright?" he asked, as we stepped into the elevator. With only four floors, this would be a much shorter awkward ride.

"I'm okay."

"Hey, don't worry." He reached out and squeezed my hand. "I'm sure Manny's doing even better, and he'll be happy to see you."

A few turns later, we approached the room labeled "Emanuel Jefferson." I couldn't remember the last time I used Manny's real name. Tapping lightly on the door, I walked in.

Alexis rose from the navy recliner to hug me. Her black Aurbor Grove University shirt clung to her petite, full figure. She wrapped a blanket around her shoulders and returned to the seat pushed against Manny's bed.

"I'm glad you made it." She patted the bed. "He tried to stay up for ya'll, but they gave him some good drugs earlier."

Manny peacefully slept under the crisp white sheet and

blankets, his chest rising and falling. I touched his cheek with my palm, his smooth skin warm against my cool hand.

I don't know what I'd expected to see, but he looked the same as he during his visit to Atlanta months ago. Same thick eyebrows, flat nose, and neatly trimmed goatee. The flimsy, gray hospital gown left the starfish-shaped birthmark on his shoulder exposed. When I turned 18, I got a tattoo exactly like it, so we'd match.

"He looks good. How is he?"

"Oh, girl he's fine."

"But you said something about a heart attack and tests. What were the results? What did the doctors say about that?"

"Gas."

At that, Jackson erupted with laughter. "Wooow."

"It was just gas." Alexis shook her head. "They said sometimes people think they're having a heart attack."

"Wait, what?" All of that built-up fear, anger, worry, anxiety, sadness poured out in non-stop giggles. My face warmed and happy tears rimmed my eyes. I fought to catch my breath and speak.

"I never, *never* in my life would have thought that."

"Me either! I watched this guy go all Fred Sanford on me," Jackson said, mimicking Redd Foxx's fake heart attack shtick from *Sanford and Son*. Taking on a froggy, raspy voice, he staggered toward the hospital bed. "*Elizabeth, I'm comin'.*" He clasped one hand against his heart and raised his other arm to the ceiling, capturing the character perfectly. "'*This is the big one!*' That's how this guy was acting earlier. Had me about to have a heart attack."

I cracked up. "He had both of us!"

Manny's eyes flickered open at our lively chatter.

"What are ya'll crows cackling about?" he asked, his voice hoarse and low.

"Oh, sorry about that, man. We were talking about your 'diagnosis,'" Jackson said, making air quotes.

"Hey, baby, do you wanna sit up?" Alexis pressed a button on the remote, and the bed whirred until he was upright. She picked up a plastic pitcher and poured him a fresh cup of water.

"You gave us a huge scare, big brother. But gas?"

"Look, it's easy to joke about it now. I've never felt chest pains like that. How do I know the difference?" He glanced behind me at Jackson. "Thanks for getting this goofball home safely, bro."

"Of course."

"I'm curious..." Manny took a dramatic sip of water, smacking his lips. "Did she drop a few choice words when you showed up?"

"Yep, you are doing fine," I said, thumping Manny's shoulder.

"Ouch! Be careful. I'm an invalid."

"Why do they still have you in here? I would've given you a dose of the pink stuff and sent your butt home."

"See that's why you're not a doctor."

"It wasn't the gas that took him out, but the tumble did," Alexis said. She flipped the end of the sheet away, revealing a wrapped splint. "He broke his leg pretty bad."

"Sis, you know I've always been clumsy."

"True. I'm surprised you made it this far in life without breaking anything."

"They said that he may need surgery." Alexis' eyebrows knitted together in concern.

"It's going to be okay," Manny said, speaking directly to

Alexis. "There's only a *chance* for surgery. And if I have to go under the knife, they say it's routine. No big deal."

"All of this for gas?" Jackson tsked. "But, hold up, I saw you up there. You were busy checking Facebook."

"No, I wasn't. I was reading my messages."

I frowned. "And what kind of text message distracted you so much that you forgot you were standing on a ladder?"

"I had a real good reason." He and Alexis exchanged silly looks. These two very grown adults acted like kids caught passing "Do you like me? Yes or No" notes in class.

"What?" Jackson and I asked at the same time.

"Well," Alexis began, rubbing her palms up and down her thighs. "I found out we're expecting."

"What!" I squealed.

Manny winked and stuck out his tongue. "Sis, you're finally gonna be an Auntie."

CHAPTER SIX

"*I*'m glad we found out about my niece so early. This will give me plenty of time to plan the shower. But instead of pink, I'm thinking we can do rose gold."

"Wait, hold up, how are you so sure it's going to be a girl?" Manny asked.

"I just have a good feeling."

Jackson smiled at me. "You think she's going to be a girly-girl or tomboy like you?"

"Nah, my baby girl is not going to be rough and tumble like Ebony."

"That's right. She's going to be just like her mama," Alexis said, yawning. "All I needed was my Barbie dolls and Easy Bake oven, and my parents could leave me all by myself for hours."

Manny looked over at Alexis. "Girl or boy, I would kind of like for my kids to play outside like we did. We had some good times."

"Do you remember how your Aunt Rosa Mae fussed at us about going back and forth in her house? '*You either need to stay in or out!'"* Jackson squinted and wagged his finger like my Aunt did when we were kids.

She had a lot of rules, but Aunt Rosa Mae had the biggest yard for us to play in and get all dirtied up before we needed a cold drink or snack.

I touched my forehead. "Goodness, I feel terrible. I haven't seen Auntie Rosa Mae since...I don't know when. How is she?"

"She's good. Still the same. Bossing me around even though she has her own business to run," Manny said. "Sometimes she cooks some of the food we serve at the Inn. Do you remember her famous cinnamon rolls?" Manny hummed, and his eyes became slits.

"Who could forget those cinnamon rolls?" Just mentioning them, I could smell the cinnamon and taste the warm, flaky layers. "I wouldn't mind having one of those right now."

"Alexis got the recipe and tried to make them herself one time. Baby tell them about how you messed up—" Manny began, turning to Alexis.

She'd curled up in the recliner and dozed off as we reminisced. Wrapped up like a mummy, only the tangle of wild, curly hair poked from the navy throw.

"I guess it has been a long day for her. For all of us."

"We probably should go," Jackson said, looking at me. "Trina said she wouldn't harass us during her shift. I can't speak for the next nurse."

So that was her name? I liked calling her Nurse Betty better.

"I'm so glad you're home. I wasn't sure if this knucklehead could get you back here."

"Hey, that's not how you presented it to me. You told me I was the only one that could make it happen."

"I said that? I must've hit my head when I fell too," Manny said, snickering. "I had to get your confidence up."

Nurse Betty squeaked open the door, peeking in.

"Hey ya'll, could I borrow Jackson for a few minutes?" she asked, ogling at him like he was the only person in the room.

As soon as Jackson excused himself, I said, "She has him on a tight leash."

"You sound jealous."

"No way. She's at work — doesn't she have patients? I think it's weird."

Manny shifted in the bed. "You don't have to worry about that. Jackson is single, and he has only one type. *She* is not it."

"Oh really, now?"

"The only woman he's thinking about tonight is you," he said, stabbing my arm with his finger. "He's been staring at you the whole time."

I shooed him away. "That's ancient history."

"Oh, so you mean to tell me you've got a line waiting for you these days? Or is he too small-time for you, now?"

"Chill out. I'm doing just fine. And I go out."

"On dates?"

"Sometimes," I mumbled. The lie refused to boldly come out.

Manny rolled his eyes. "Really, now? Last time we talked, you told me you hadn't met anyone since you and the doctor-I-told-you-never-to-date broke up a year ago."

"There you go bringing up old stuff." I playfully punched him.

"Ouch," he winced, grabbing his shoulder.

"I barely touched you."

"I guess it's true. Hurt people hurt people," he laughed.

"Stop playing around. Me and Jackson are friends. The only reason I haven't been dating is because I've been focused on — "

"On your career. I know. But there's more to life than work, sis."

That stung. So much for sharing my 'good news' about my promotion.

I folded my arms and shook my head. "Don't say it like that. Like it's all I care about."

"You know I love you, and only want the best. And you and Jackson together always made my life easier. My man has had a bad run with the ladies ever since you left him."

"I didn't leave him...exactly." I drew my shoulder to my ear and threw my hands up.

Manny side-eyed me. "You do realize I was there, right?"

"Okay, but it wasn't all because of him. I left you, everybody, and everything after..."

I still couldn't form the words. Years later, the painful memory refused to roll off my tongue without stammering. Without me feeling the pitter-patter of my heart quicken to the point I could barely breathe.

"All I'm saying is, since you broke up with him, either the woman isn't good enough, or something crazy goes down."

"Like what?" I was curious and amused at the same time.

"You know Karen Wright from high school?"

"Hmm. She was pretty unforgettable."

"Right! She had the biggest –"

As Manny was about to dish out the juicy details, Jackson returned and we suddenly hushed. My eyes fell to the green and white checkered floor.

"Were ya'll talking about me?"

39

"Yep." Manny nodded his head. "I was telling her about your latest dating disaster."

Jackson glanced at me, then back at Manny. "On that note, I'm going downstairs and warm up the truck."

I raised an eyebrow at his abrupt exit. "I guess that's my cue to leave."

"Sounds like it."

I gave Manny another hug and kissed his forehead. When I pulled away, he held on to my elbow.

"Look, I desperately need your help at the Inn. I don't know about this surgery thing, but if I have to have it, I'm going to be in here a little longer than I want," he said. "I can only imagine the hospital bill I'm racking up, so we can't afford to close up shop. Not now."

"Sure, I can help however."

"Alexis printed out this week's schedule and has instructions for everything we do in that binder." He pointed toward a large 3-ring binder sticking out of Alexis' crimson leather purse.

"My wife ain't no joke. She explains everything step-by-step."

"Is it really that complicated? I figure people give me their ID and credit card and I give them a room key."

"It's simple but a lot of our guests are loyal customers – we like to take care of them like family. That's why they come back to us again and again."

Our parents preached the "like family" message when the Inn first opened. They had this idea of attracting people from all over the world and turning them into family. I always thought inviting strangers into our most personal space was a crazy notion, but Manny carried on the mantra of our parents.

"I can handle that."

"I don't know, you've been in the big city so long, your customer service skills might be a little shaky," Manny said, making a jittery hand motion.

"Stop acting like I never worked at the Inn before."

"We have some folks comin' in town for the Jingle Bell Festival, but the Rose Room is open. You can crash there or in our apartment."

"I don't want to be all up in your business, so I'll take the Rose Room," I said, patting his shoulder. "You don't have to worry about anything except getting well. Once you get home, I'll get Alexis to take me back to Atlanta."

"You're not staying for Christmas?"

I jerked my head back. "Oh, God, no. I thought this was a weekend thing."

Manny huffed a sigh of annoyance.

"Why not? You haven't been home for years — you can't stay for a few days?"

I played with the bedsheet, fidgeting over the rough, cotton fabric, avoiding his peering eyes. I knew my true feelings would offend him, but I spoke them anyway. "Manny, this isn't home for me anymore."

"That's wrong. This will always be home," he said, his voice catching in his throat. "Always."

I clamped my lips shut, unsure of what else to say. I felt the emotion bubbling up inside of him, and didn't want to make things worse.

"Okay I'm going to go." I leaned down to hug him, and he stopped me. He reached for my necklace swinging in front of him, catching the cross in his palm.

"Is this the same necklace Mama gave you?" he asked, a mix of shock and somberness in his voice.

"Yep. Sweet 16." I smiled as the joy and warmth of the memory rushed over me. Transported back to that day when I unwrapped the box and laid eyes on the silver necklace I didn't know I needed. It had been the nicest gift I'd ever received. Real jewelry, not the cheap, costume stuff I bought at the mall. And it matched the same necklace my mother wore daily.

"I remember. You kept it after all these years?"

"I wear it every day too. Just like Mama did."

Manny's mood abruptly shifted, and he averted his eyes. I couldn't tell what he was thinking. Between refusing to spend the holidays with him and bringing up Mama, I don't know which upset him the most.

Why was I always disappointing the people I loved?

"Well, I don't want to keep Jackson waiting."

"Yeah, that's right," he said, shaking his head like he'd forgotten all about him. All about how he'd put my homecoming into motion. "Take the binder and read over everything. If you have any questions, call us."

"Manny, relax. I manage events – *huge events* – for a living. I'm sure I can figure this out."

CHAPTER SEVEN

"*I* don't think I can figure this out," I mumbled. In the passenger seat of Jackson's truck, I leafed through Alexis' multi-tabbed, color-coded binder full of sheet-protected checklists and directions. Manny wasn't lying about her attention to detail.

Jackson rested his hand on the gear, leaning over to peek at the open binder.

"Ha, I see you've been introduced to the Alexis method."

"It's a method alright," I said. "And I thought I was Type-A."

"Yeah, I think ya'll might be two sides of the same coin."

"What do you mean?"

"You've always had the perfect plan for *everything*. I was so scared on prom night, I read your checklist fifty-'leven times."

I laughed along with him. It sounded ridiculous now, but at the time, I wanted to make sure everything was special. So, yes, I prepared an itinerary and to-do list!

"You're laughing, but guess what? It was a perfect night."

"True. But that's not why it was perfect for me," he said. "If I remember correctly, we had a few hiccups."

"Because you forgot to fill up the car."

"It wasn't on your list!"

"Messing around with your bootlegged jug, you had me walking in there smelling like gas." I covered my mouth, my whole body shaking with laughter.

"And it didn't matter one bit. I just wanted to be with you."

My laughter stuttered into a goofy smile that mirrored his. Lost in the memory, he acted like it was normal to say things like that with such certainty. He didn't hold any of the doubts I lugged around and for a moment I wished I could be like him. To care for him like he cared for me, without question. It seemed like all I had to hang onto sometimes were questions.

What if he was only saying this to make me feel better?

My silent pondering caught his attention.

"What? It's true," he said, reading my mind again. The silly smile faded, replaced with longing. He gazed at me a beat too long —oh, we definitely weren't just thinking about the 'good ole days' anymore.

Suddenly, the smoldering intensity from him and the heat pouring from the air vents became too much.

"Whew, okay." I broke away from his mesmerizing glare and removed my coat. "Okay, okay, I may have been a little too much, but listen," I said, flipping through sections in Alexis' book. I steered the conversation back to my original point and away from me. Away from us.

"She has a tab called 'Bathroom Protocol' with a rule about the tissue being rolled over, not under, and folded to a point."

"I have never in my life thought about that," Jackson said, snickering.

I closed the binder. "I'll have to finish this tomorrow because it's too much for one night."

"Well, let me get you home so you can get plenty of rest before your first day on the job." He pulled off slowly, then turned onto the highway.

"Oh, I didn't pack anything to wear. Can you take me somewhere to buy some clothes first?"

"At this hour?" He sighed. "I think even Walmart is closed."

"I forgot how early everything shuts down around this town."

"I can take you shopping in the morning," he said. One hand on the steering wheel, he reached in the back seat and grabbed a duffle bag. "I have a clean sweatshirt and jogging pants if you want to at least get comfortable tonight."

"Ugh."

"There was a time when you were proud to wear my stuff."

My face burned, but I let that comment slide. All these thoughts of *us* were too much to process alongside everything else shifting in my life. My emotions — excitement at my promotion, anxiety about Manny falling, sadness over memories of my parents, and complete confusion over Jackson — wrestled all day and night. I was exhausted from all the back and forth.

I wanted to focus on Manny getting better and me getting back to normal in Atlanta.

My brother's words ricocheted in my mind.

This will always be home.

"Everything seems so much smaller now," I muttered.

Unlike Atlanta's poles and buildings casting artificial light, the stars and moon shined brightest in Aurbor Grove. Not that there was much to see anyway.

There was a lot of in-progress construction and signs advertising future, expensive condos. I recognized a few locations that had been around when I was a child. Darkness blanketed the low, flat businesses, and a lot of vacant buildings dotted the streets. The plant where seemingly everyone I knew worked at now had planks across the windows and an overgrown front field.

Jackson pointed out places from our past—the park we played at, the old elementary school, and spots that looked like nothing now. Only our memories of what used to be there remained.

"Have you ever thought about leaving?" I asked.

"Sure, I have. But it's home."

He sounded like Manny, pronouncing the word with a fervor I never possessed.

"I like being close to family, and the tight-knit community feel."

I rolled my eyes, chortling, "Where everybody's in your business?"

"Or," he said, raising a finger. "Willing to lend a helping hand. Word traveled so fast about Manny falling. We were lucky to squeeze in after hours. Trina told me that he had visitors almost non-stop — friends, family. I mean any and everybody checked on him and Alexis. They had to turn people away."

I see Nurse Betty was like everybody else — always watching every move and ready to report it all. By the time I woke up in the morning, everyone would know I'd returned. Yep, the prodigal daughter had come back.

The thought of having to explain myself, my choices,

and my absence was too heavy a burden. That's why I had zero plans to see or talk to anybody except Manny and Alexis. I wanted to get in and out.

"They were probably being nosy as usual."

"Some of them, maybe. But it's nice to live somewhere you know people have your back," he said. "Plus I love the work I do. I'm not bringing home big bucks or anything, but it's more than most."

"You could be making even more at a law firm in Atlanta," I said. "And if I recall correctly, the Jackson I knew had bigger plans. You still interested in politics?"

"Maybe. I don't know. I do a lot of work with the county. There are some things happening around here that need improving, but people are scared to speak out. I'm not."

"I can see that too. You always were a troublemaker."

"Only the good kind of trouble," he said. "I could probably move somewhere else, but this feels right. As my Mom and Pops get older, I want to be near them."

I brushed away the pang inside at the mention of his still-living parents.

I'd probably still be here if...

"Do you ever think of coming back?"

"Never." His jaw clenched at my answer. He didn't say anything but I felt like I needed to defend myself anyway. "I love my job too. I actually got a promotion tonight."

"Oh wow. Congratulations."

"You're the only person I've told."

"Why didn't you tell Manny?"

"I don't know. Technically, I haven't accepted the offer yet. And my good news in light of his broken leg and baby news – I didn't want to overshadow him."

Once we passed Aunt Rosa Mae's café, I knew we were only a few blocks away from what used to be my home.

I took a deep breath, bracing myself.

WELCOME TO THE AURBOR GROVE INN!
Our home is your home.

Manny maintained the same rustic sign Daddy had custom-made by a friend who enjoyed wood-working. He had attached red, velvet bows at each end of the stained cedar wood.

Jackson pulled into the long driveway, gravel crackling underneath. The two-story white house with black shutters came into view. While everything else in Aurbor Grove appeared so small, our house seemed much bigger than I remembered.

Christmas lights rung around the four large columns and along the upstairs front balcony. A jolly Santa sat waving on top of the roof, but only two reindeer trotted out in front of him.

Jackson jogged over to open the truck door and help me out. Tall plastic candy canes lined the perfectly landscaped pathway to the front door. The rocking chairs on the wrap-around porch held square, black pillows with the Inn's logo stitched on the front.

As Jackson opened the door, little golden bells dangling from the large wreath jingled.

He handed the keys to me. "You can have my extra set. Alexis has them labeled."

Warmth and the scent of apple cinnamon greeted us in the foyer. I hung my jacket on the coat hanger and flipped on the lights. Manny and Alexis had upgraded the furniture and fixtures, but for the most part everything was the same. I spotted poinsettias throughout the sitting room. Garland and ivory stockings framed the fireplace.

They were much nicer than the tattered ones that had held me and Manny's names.

Open Christmas cards and framed photos from long ago crowded the mantle. I think I spied a picture of all of us at prom — me, Jackson, Manny, and Alexis.

Memories of the room swirled like an emotional tornado inside. Maybe sleep would bring me peace.

Well as long as I didn't find myself fantasizing about Jackson again.

I reached for his bag of clothes and my stuff, stopping Jackson in the foyer.

"It's okay if you leave my things here. Thanks again for everything."

He hesitated, but eventually handed it all over.

"Alright, see you tomorrow," I said, brightly. It was good-bye, but he didn't move. He stood there, hands stuffed in his black leather jacket pockets, staring at me.

The heat of his glare made me so nervous, I tried to laugh it off. "Stop it."

"I'm sorry. I just want to say it's nice to have you home."

My lips parted, but no words came out. I didn't know what to say. Finally, I said what I thought I *should* say, whether I believed it or not: "It's good to be home."

"Took long enough. I hate something bad had to happen for you to come back."

I should have let it go. Or relented and invited him in for hot chocolate and more stories about the past. But his statement irritated me.

Did he think I would not show up for my family?

What did he mean by 'took long enough?'

"Look, Jackson, I know we haven't seen each other since..." My words trailed off, catching in my throat. "I'm here to take care of my brother. I don't want things to be weird between us."

"Who's being weird?"

"You pretend like nothing's changed. But *everything* has changed," I said, raising my voice. "When you bring up how we used to be or talk about me leaving, it makes me feel like you're still mad at me about what happened."

"It's not that. I'm not mad at you."

"Well, what's the problem?"

His amber irises dimmed. I could tell he wanted to say more, but he knew he'd already said too much. And me being me, I had to hit back.

"I didn't ask you to come pick me up. That was on you," I snapped.

In that second I *heard* myself, and I didn't like me. I knew exactly what I was doing. I was picking a fight. If Jackson wouldn't pull away, I'd push him myself.

He took a step forward. I thought he was going to hug me, but he shrugged instead. "You're right. And I'm glad I did. I shouldn't have said it like that, but you know what I mean."

That was the thing about wounds like mine — innocent or careless words picked at the scab, triggering the sting of injury all over again.

"I don't know what you want from me."

"I'm not gonna stand here and lie. I would like to know what happened between us. How you could leave like that and then nothing. What did I do wrong?" He held up his palms in a surrender motion. "And I'm talking about back then. You never told me why."

"Can we leave the past in the past and move on?"

"I get it," he said. "Bad things happened here. But good

things happened here too. Do you want to ignore that? What we had?"

"I don't remember it being all that good."

He scrunched his face, turning away. *What was that washing over him? Regret? A flash of anger that he didn't want me to see?*

I pressed my hand so hard against my chest, willing my heart to calm down, that I felt the outline of my cross necklace.

I remembered.

But there were so many words left unsaid for too many years, we couldn't simply pick up where we ended. The reasons didn't sound right anymore, so I didn't offer them.

I reached up, cradled his chin in my hand, forcing him to look at me. "All you talk about is what we had. I don't want to ruin what we have left."

"What exactly do we have left?" Jackson's eyes bored into me, that wall cracking as the seconds ticked by.

"You can't think of anything?" His question came out more like a plea. A final attempt to get me to remember.

I fidgeted with the cross, running my finger along its sharp edge.

"Our friendship. That's all we have."

"Okay, then. Friends it is." He nodded solemnly, biting his bottom lip.

"I'm sorry."

"No need to apologize. Good night, Ebony."

When he pulled the door closed, the slam echoed throughout the empty house. He was gone, but the thick tension weighed heavy all around me.

I scratched the hair at the nape of my neck, working my fingers around to the chain of my necklace. Watching Jackson from the window next to the door, his blurry figure receded. The engine of his truck growled to life, blinding yellow headlights lit up the yard, then there was nothing except darkness and my own face looking back at me.

I'd lied. To myself and Jackson.

I hadn't forgotten about us. And I didn't want to be alone. But I had been operating in independent mode for so long, I couldn't bring myself to admit otherwise. Especially not to him.

CHAPTER EIGHT

*I*t didn't matter that I tossed and turned until 2 am, my body woke up at 7am.

I typically spent the first half-hour scrolling through e-mails and downing my first cup of coffee.

At the Inn, I didn't want to leave the soft sleigh bed and warmth of the down comforter. The birds chirping outside the window almost lulled me back to sleep.

I propped myself up on one elbow, light peeking in between the pulled curtains. I took in the updated decor of the smallest room at the Inn. A funky lamp stood in the sitting area between two dark red chairs. If you sat there, you could look out the three windows and take in the sprawling backyard garden.

Manny and Alexis kept my mother's large framed painting of deep red roses hanging on the mauve wall.

When the doorbell rang, I ignored it. I was up, but not *up-up*. Besides, check-in wasn't until 3 pm. Whoever decided to pop up unannounced would have to come again at a decent hour.

My phone buzzed, an unfamiliar number across the

screen.

"Hello?"

"Good morning, sunshine." Jackson's voice was cheery and wide awake.

"Boy, are you crazy?"

"If Manny and Alexis were here, they'd be open for business."

"It's too early."

"I'm supposed to take you shopping this morning, and I am a man of my word…freezing outside your door."

I groaned. "Okay, give me a minute."

"Hurry, I got something special for you," he teased.

I caught a glimpse of myself in the mirror. My new 'do was in every direction except the right one — I raked my fingers through my hair, trying to tame the frizz.

I'd forgotten I was still dressed in Jackson's gray and black AGU jogging pants and sweatshirt. The ensemble swallowed my frame, making me look like a blob. I tried to adjust the outfit, but there was no way to make Gildan sweats stylish. I really didn't want him to see me like this, but I had no other choice. Then again the way he admired the idea of me wearing his clothes like back in the day, he'd probably enjoy seeing me in the getup.

I jogged downstairs and opened the door. A burst of cold air greeted me.

"H-hey." His eyebrows crinkled, looking me from head to toe. "You really just woke up, huh?"

"Get in this house."

Cinnamon?

Sugar?

"I know you didn't."

"I absolutely did." As if entranced by the aroma of sweet treats, I followed him into the kitchen. He pulled off the top of the pan, revealing a half-dozen of Aunt Rosa Mae's cinnamon rolls. I washed my hands, then picked up a sticky, gooey roll.

"Did you make any coffee yet?"

"No, I didn't read Alexis' instructions on coffee-making yet," I said, my mouth full of the flaky pastry.

"It's one thing she makes easy." Jackson removed his black wool coat and sauntered to a corner of the kitchen. A turnstile of several flavors of coffee and tea sat next to a machine on the granite countertop.

"You look like you could use something bold," he said, selecting a pod.

"Ha-ha."

"I'm kidding. You're a natural beauty."

"Whatever." It was too early — and before my coffee— so I couldn't think of a snarky response fast enough.

Besides, Jackson looked perfectly *fine*. In the bright light of a new day, I got a better look at him.

I didn't know it was possible to look better as you age. Maybe it was the thick, jet-black beard. That was a thing now. It added a ruggedness to his dimpled babyface. The charcoal gray sweater accentuated his muscled arms and chest, so he wasn't that lanky, lean guy anymore either.

I took another bite of the cinnamon roll to keep myself from saying something stupid.

"I felt bad about how things ended last night." He sat a cup of steaming coffee in front of me.

"You were right. I was acting weird. But it was only because I didn't think it would be like this. Between us." Jackson whipped his hand in the air. "Seeing you again brought back some feelings I thought were long gone. I needed some time to process everything."

Instead of responding, I took a big sip of coffee, burning

my tongue. *Ouch!*

"I realized that I was pushing you to feel the same way I felt. And that's not fair at all. Like you said, the past is the past. We both should move on as friends."

"Just friends," I repeated.

This was precisely what I *thought* I'd wanted to hear Jackson say, but his moment of clarity only made me more confused.

"Do you accept my apology?" he asked. The crinkle of his eyebrows and sincere eyes hypnotized me.

"I do."

He caught the irony in my matrimonial response and laughed. I slapped my forehead.

"I mean, I appreciate you saying that. And for bringing the cinnamon rolls."

"Hey, I figured you wouldn't leave me out in the cold if I came bearing gifts."

"You keep bribing me with food. I don't know what that says about me."

People always said food was a way to a man's heart. Well, it was a pretty good strategy to wiggle into this woman's heart as well.

"So, my first duty as your friend, is to take you shopping."

"How long do you have? Is today a busy day for you?"

"I don't usually work much on Saturdays," he said. "See that's the other great thing about small towns, business gets *sol-ow* for me during the holidays."

Jackson stretched out his hands, smiling from ear to ear. "I'm all yours."

I eyed him over the rim of my coffee cup, covering a slick smile tugging at my lips.

Remember, just friends.

* * *

"There's the penne pasta you were looking for." Jackson stopped pushing my Walmart shopping cart in the middle of the aisle, nearly causing a pile-up on Aisle 5.

A little old woman with blue-gray curls swerved around us, muttering some choice words under her breath.

"Merry Christmas to you too!" Jackson shouted after her, then turned to me with a *'What in the world?'* scowl.

"Don't get us into any fights in Walmart, okay?" I said, grabbing a box of pasta. I studied the nutritional facts and long list of ingredients, then selected a different brand.

He pulled our cart to the side. "I thought you were only staying a few days?"

"Yeah, that's the plan."

"Who are you feeding?" His hand hovered over the piles of food.

"Well, I thought it would be nice to cook a welcome home meal for Manny and Alexis. I'm sure they're tired of feasting on cafeteria and fast food," I said.

"I guess all of this will fit in my truck."

"Ha-ha. I'm almost done."

I was wearing my same outfit from yesterday, and couldn't wait to throw on one of the new sets of cardigans and slacks I'd found. They weren't my usual brand or style, but anything was better than Jackson's sweats.

A few random items caught my eye, so I tossed them in the overflowing cart too. Now that I knew I was going to be an Auntie, the baby section required my attention.

Ever so often, Jackson stopped to chit-chat with family, friends, different people from church, work, and wherever. That alone added another 30 minutes to our trip, but I was thankful I hadn't spotted any of my family members.

"I need some socks. That's it. I promise."

He navigated through the narrow aisles packed with all kinds of gift ideas. Despite the early time, the store buzzed with anxious shoppers, filling their baskets with Christmas decorations and presents.

Jackson threw a pack of multi-colored socks like it was a basketball.

"That's it?"

"Oh, I forgot." I snapped a finger. "I need a flat iron."

"What?" His eyes darted to the top of my head. I'd successfully pulled the bushy hair into a ponytail.

"This right here is going to be an afro tomorrow if I don't get it together."

His fingers brushed over his lip thoughtfully. "I think I'd like to see that."

"Stop playing. I want to get done with this and go see Manny."

"Nah." He smoothed his hand over my crown. "I wanna see the 'fro. And it better be a big one too. I'm talking Pam Grier-Foxy Brown big."

"Seriously?"

"Yeah." His eyes fell to mine, and he paused as if considering his words carefully. "I'm sure your natural style is the most beautiful version of you. I wanna see it."

"Whatever." I slid past him and his request. I didn't want him to see the smile of amusement fighting through or the color filling my cheeks.

Were friends supposed to flirt this much?

"I guess I could check to see if Alexis has one if it gets really bad. Alright, I'm ready to check out."

The shortest line had seven people waiting for a self-checkout station.

As Darlene Love belted out *Christmas, Baby Please Come*

Home Jackson hummed along, bobbing his head to the upbeat tune.

"This is one of my favorite songs right here. Christmas classic."

"It's alright."

"*Baby, please come home*," he sang in a flat falsetto.

"Yeah, you should never sing that out loud again."

Just as we were about to get our chance to check out, someone shouted, "Ebony Jefferson? Is that you?"

I ran my eyes across the store but didn't recognize any of the faces.

"Hey, it's me!" A woman with shoulder-length, wavy black hair and blue eyes rushed over. She bear-hugged me before I could even react. I gave Jackson a questioning look over her meaty shoulder.

He shrugged his shoulders and mouthed *I don't know who she is.*

"Oh, wow. I haven't seen you since high school. I just got in town for the holidays, and you're the first person I see. How about that?"

"Hey, yeah, um, crazy, right?" I stammered, forcing a big smile. "It's good to see you too."

She turned and noticed Jackson. Her jaw dropped and she grabbed his arm. "Oh my goodness. This is so sweet. Ya'll are still together?" she drawled.

"Well, we—"

"No, you see—"

We both talked over her, attempting to stop this train wreck of a reunion, but Blue Eyes wasn't having it.

"I knew ya'll were going to make it. I just knew it. Ya'll were perfect for each other. And if I'm being honest I was a little jealous..."

"It's not like that—" I began, trying to hush her up again.

"...Most high school relationships don't last. Mine didn't. Chet dumped me right after graduation. Remember that? I met my husband in college, so..."

Jackson stepped between me and her. He raised his voice so loud, she jerked. "You know what, we'd love to continue to catch up with you, but I have an appointment."

"Oh, oh. Okay. I understand." She reached out for another hug. "Have a Merry Christmas!"

Still clueless about who she was, we both burst into laughter, shoulders quaking.

"I could not get a word in at all," Jackson said.

"Poor thing. She thinks we..."

Made it, I finished the sentence in my head.

"Ah, you can't let that bother you. People make assumptions all the time," he said.

"I'm not bothered. Just another adventure in your hometown Walmart, right?"

Jackson didn't answer right away, mumbling a beat later, "Right."

I returned to sliding my items across the self-checkout register. With each scan, *Beep!* peppered the heavy silence between us. A tingling sensation rippled through me as Jackson watched me. I robotically handed off each item for him to bag and load into the cart.

I couldn't escape it. *Us. Together.*

Not in my dreams.

Not in my home.

Not in a simple trip to the grocery store.

It seemed like it didn't matter if we agreed it was best to be just friends. Everything and everyone else pushed us together.

And all of it made me wonder if I made the wrong decision then...and now.

CHAPTER NINE

$\mathcal{T}$he rest of the weekend, I intentionally only called Jackson to take me to visit Manny. We needed space and time apart. Those first couple of days together were too much too fast.

I had to devote all of my energy to focusing on my reason for being here. Manny needed surgery and would likely be on crutches for weeks. He and Alexis asked me to stay a little longer until the doctor approved his release.

As eager as I was to get back home, I wanted the Inn to be one less thing for them to worry about as he began to recover. I couldn't commit to weeks, but I could give them a few days to settle back in.

Despite the news about surgery, they were most concerned about the customers that'd booked rooms for the Jingle Bell Festival. I assured them I had it all under control and would have everything ready.

A few hours from the first check-in, I held Alexis' massive handbook in arm, reading each line of her checklist.

The private bathroom was stocked with natural soaps,

shampoo, plush towels, and sparkling clean with the faint smell of lavender.

I reviewed the customer profile.

A couple. Elle Shepherd and Jared Owen booked the Sunflower Suite for a week. My jaw dropped when I saw the note: *Eloping. Make it special.*

What did that mean?

I called Alexis. "Hey, I had a question about the check-in, Elle and Jared. The elopers...is that a word? Anyway, you have a note about making it special."

"Oh, yeah, I totally forgot. They met at the Inn last year and are getting married in the garden. There's really nothing you need to do, except make sure it looks good. As a gift, I got them monogrammed towels that I wanted to put in their room as a special touch," she said, the sound of the hospital intercom coming through the phone. "They're in our apartment somewhere. I think Manny left them in the hallway closet."

"Okay, I'll look and be sure to hang them before they check in."

"I wanted to give you a heads-up, don't worry about preparing breakfast for them. It's not that we don't trust your cooking, we thought it would be easier to order from Aunt Rosa Mae. She'll have it delivered by 8:30."

"You're not going to hear any complaining from me. I had some of her rolls and don't know how I've lived this long without them."

"Oh, you went to the cafe?"

"No, Jackson brought them by."

"Ya'll didn't mention that you had breakfast together," Alex sang. "Interesting."

"Don't get started."

"I'm not saying nothing. I just said *interesting*."

"Yeah, yeah. I know what you're thinking."

"That you two are gonna get back together, settle down and get married, have some babies and babysit this rascal I got coming along when me and Manny have date night?" She ticked off her own fantasy that surprisingly sounded similar to the one I'd dreamed of, but knew was impossible. "Nah, I wasn't thinking that."

I bounded down the steps to Manny and Alexis' apartment. They had modernized the space I grew up in with my parents once they converted our house to a bed-and-breakfast.

Instead of linoleum, they'd installed a glossy flooring and painted over the wood paneling to create more of a chic farmhouse look.

It was obvious they'd left their home with intentions to come back and finish tidying up. Dirty dishes tossed in the sink. Shoes scattered on the floor. The satellite TV had gone off automatically. A message about pressing "Start" to watch bounced from corner to corner.

I turned the TV OFF, picked up a few items, and put the dishes in the washer.

The door to the hallway closet was halfway open. Packed with an old vacuum, tools, clothes, and boxes, finding this gift bag might be a bigger challenge than I'd expected.

Old photo albums, dusty record albums, and a bag full of bags crowded the corners. Alexis and Manny hadn't cleaned this thing out in years—if anything, they tossed more crap in all willy-nilly.

A bright red bag smashed between a VCR/DVD combo machine and old romance books stacked on the top shelf caught my eye. That had to be the wedding gift. The weight was off when I grabbed the bag.

Instead of towels, composition notebooks were inside. I

recognized the tattered edges and scribbling on the covers. These were my journals. Unlike most girls my age, instead of keeping a diary of my deepest secrets, I meticulously wrote out plans for my day, week, month, year, a whole lifetime.

I opened the notebook and read the words on the yellowing, blue-lined pages. The me before I lost my parents was so optimistic about living in Aurbor Grove forever.

Ironic, huh?

For so long, I could only recall the younger me who lost it all. Intrigued by this version of myself I'd forgotten about, I sat on the sofa and read for a whole hour.

One thing that was almost on target was my dream of planning events—although back then, I was into weddings. Or specifically, "becoming the best wedding planner in the whole United States."

Oh, I aimed high even as a teenager.

According to the journal, not only did I HAVE to get a 3.5 to get into Aurbor Grove University, but I wanted to be a mom of twins and marry Jackson after he finished law school. In case my written words didn't fully capture my love for him, I'd drawn a string of hearts around Jackson's name.

Love notes from him were stashed between pages. Rereading them unearthed feelings I'd buried deep down.

"We're just friends," I reminded myself. "Just friends."

'Just friends was the safest route, but I didn't have 'just friends' type thoughts all the time.

Let me put it this way. Everybody has a "what-if" ex. You know, the one you wonder *what if we'd stayed together*? You imagine how your life would be different and, in your mind, you can only see the happily ever after. We would probably be married. Maybe a couple kids. He'd have his successful law firm, and I'd have my events company. Our love for each other and our families would be so strong. Barbecues at the house. Double date nights with Manny and Alexis.

Yep, Jackson Oliver was my what-if ex.

That's what made being around him so dangerous. He got my mind wondering, and my heart wandering. His presence made me question my choices.

A dull ache had settled in my bones as soon as he crossed my office threshold. I needed Jackson. I didn't realize it before he came to pick me up, and I hated knowing it now because I knew we couldn't be together.

My eyes stung at the memory of the promise I'd made. I slammed the journal shut.

Seeing the life I *could've* lived stirred a deep sadness within. Suddenly, I felt all alone in this world.

No Jackson. No twins.

It's just me.

I jumped at the trill of my phone.

Alexis: Did you find the towels?

Her text message reminded me of my original reason for coming downstairs. I went back to the closet and tucked those journals and the feelings they spurred away. I spotted a recyclable Target bag with the towels. I ran my hands over the monogrammed initials: EOJ.

Those were the same letters for Jackson and me. While we didn't get far in the wedding planning, that was something we'd played around with.

A loud bang drew my attention away. I rushed upstairs, taking two steps at a time.

The kitchen, den, and sunroom were all empty. The crash sounded again, and I realized the ruckus came from outside. Rushing out without a coat, I noticed Jackson's white truck. I followed the noise to the roof.

"What are you doing?"

I could not escape this man.

"Oh, hey," Jackson said, shading his eyes with a hand. "I came to finish the decorations."

"Don't you have some clients or work to do?" I shouted.

"The Jingle Bell Festival is tomorrow, and they judge early in the morning."

I'd forgotten we were participating in the decoration competition.

I folded my arms across my chest, biting the inside of my jaw. Jackson here, *again,* made me feel claustrophobic. I didn't have the space to think through everything. But this was important to Manny and Alexis — so much so, he landed in the hospital. And I couldn't complete the job, so there it was again...I needed Jackson.

"You can do that all by yourself? I can't afford to have both of ya'll in the hospital."

"Trust me. Plus I left my phone in the truck." He winked at me and continued to work.

"Alright. Holler if you need me."

I left him and prepped the Sunflower Suite for Elle and Jared.

By the time Jackson finished, I'd checked in our happy couple and chatted with them about their plans in the den.

Per the rulebook, I offered them macaroons and tea.

"These things right here," Jared began, holding up the soft, red velvet cookie. "They're reason enough to keep coming back."

Both of them praised Manny and Alexis' thoughtfulness.

"I stumbled on the Inn last year. I was working crazy hours and completely burnt out. I wanted to go somewhere I didn't know anyone and could hit reset," Jared said. "I felt like I left with a brother, sister, well and a new girlfriend."

"You'll probably think I'm a terrible person," Elle began, covering her pie-shaped face with her hands, "but I was with my boyfriend when I met Jared. Things were rocky, and we hoped getting away for a few days would give our relationship new life."

"In her and my defense, the guy was a total jerk," Jared interrupted.

"He spent the whole time working. When we were supposed to be reconnecting, I was by myself most of the time," Elle said. "Jared liked sitting in the garden too, so we'd see each other every day."

"On the last day, I got up the nerve to ask for her number. And here we are back again."

Elle and Jared looked at each other, blushing.

"Wow, that's a love story. We need to feature you two on the website," I said. Ideas of how Manny could market customer stories like these popped up in my mind.

"We figured this was the best place for us to get married."

"I have to admit I'm a little bummed that Manny and Alexis won't be here. We'd wanted them as our witnesses," Jared said. He snapped his finger. "You can stand in for them, though."

"Um, I don't know about that."

"No, it's really simple," Elle said. "We're doing a short ceremony in the gardens. It's easy. Just stand there and smile."

"Could you do that for us? It would mean a lot to us."

A list of excuses came to mind, but I also thought of what Manny and Alexis would do. They wanted to make things 'special,' so that's what I would have to do—treat them like family.

"Alright. I'll be there."

"Yay!" Elle cheered, reaching over to hug me. "Are you going to the Jingle Bell Festival? It's the closest thing to a bachelorette and bachelor party we're having. I know, lame, but we enjoy it."

"Truthfully, I hadn't considered it. I'll probably hang around the house."

"Oh, you've got to go," Jared said.

"He's right. It's a tradition," Jackson chimed in. He'd cleaned up, changing into a sweater and jeans. "You have to represent the Inn on Manny's behalf."

Three pairs of eyes fell on me. I'm usually not a sucker for peer pressure, but it wasn't like I had anything else to do.

"I guess I can check it out for a few minutes."

CHAPTER TEN

The Main Street Square glowed with white lights around poles, lush green wreaths with red bows, and every business went above and beyond with decorations.

Jackson and I walked, hand-in-hand, visiting various vendors and businesses as Christmas tunes blared.

All of the beautiful decorations, sounds, and cheerful people kneaded away the knots inside me. I relaxed. Breathed a little slower. Let my shoulders drop. Although it all brought memories of my parents to the forefront like ghosts of Christmas past, I didn't feel that heaviness as much.

I still wished they were here too, but for the first time in a long time, I was happy to be here. Being home actually felt good and had yet to live up to all of the bad emotions and happenings I'd conjured in my mind.

Jackson bought us a funnel cake to share, but the way my sweet tooth is set up, I'd eaten more than half, getting powdered sugar everywhere.

"Do you remember the last time we came to the Jingle Bell Festival together?" Jackson asked.

I squinted my eyes, mentally flipping through the years. I shook my head, drawing a blank.

"You're too young to be this forgetful. Anyway, it was like a Christmas miracle because we actually got snow."

"Oh, yes! Now I remember. It didn't stick, but we tried our best to make snow angels," I said, breaking up in laughter. "We were like two big kids out there."

"It was more like an ice and grass mess!"

"Just a mess."

"So, did you decide on the job yet?"

"What?" I'd not only forgotten about my much-coveted promotion but that I'd shared the news with Jackson. "I'm still thinking about it."

Jackson pulled off a piece of the cake, frowning at me. "The Ebony I know is pretty decisive. What's the hold-up?"

"It pushes me to the next level, which I like the pay and stuff, but it's managing people. That's it. I won't get to do what I love anymore."

"Then you shouldn't take it."

"It's not that simple."

"You're an ambitious person, but I know you also want to be happy. I see people all the time climbing that ladder and then when they get to the top, they realize they never really wanted what was up there to begin with."

I thought about my journals, comparing the dream with my reality.

"You used to talk about doing your own thing all the time. With all the experience you've racked up, you could open your own event planning company," he said.

"I've thought about it, but starting a business is so risky. Most entrepreneurs fail within the first year."

"Stop doubting yourself. Look at all the successful business owners you have in your family. They've been around for years."

"True."

He pecked my forehead with a kiss. "Think about that."

"Aha, you just wanted to sneak that in."

"I was smooth, right?"

"Not at all." I playfully pushed him off the sidewalk.

As a chorus group took the stage to sing carols, we inched in closer to the crowd gathering on the courtyard. In perfect harmony, they sang a rendition of 'O Holy Night.' That was my mom's favorite Christmas song. She couldn't hit the notes, but she tried anyway, claiming that it wasn't the tune that mattered, but the words.

"...*thrill of hope, the weary world rejoices...*" I sang quietly along, each lyric a balm to this heart of mine. Jackson must have sensed what was happening within me, gripping my hand tighter, humming along.

After the group went through a few more songs, the mayor took the stage. He bragged on how the community came together every year for the special occasion.

"Our Annual Jingle Bell Festival is more than a time to have fun and enjoy the sites and scenes of our beautiful town. It's a chance to connect, neighbor with neighbor," he said. He swooped the few strands of hair he had left across the shiny bald cul-de-sac on his head.

"It's also a time to get creative and showcase our Christmas spirit. Each year we award "Best Decorations," and this year, I must say the competition was tough."

"Do you think we're gonna win?" I asked.

"We have a good chance. Last year, Manny won, and he had only half the lights and no rooftop scenery."

The mayor waved a card in the air. "I have our official

winners. Our third-place award goes to Bourbon Street Bistro, for their New Orleans inspired look."

A smattering of applause followed as the head Chef took the stage to thank his staff.

"For second place, we have the Main Street Froyo & Ice-cream Shoppe." The husband and wife owners jogged to the stage to accept their trophy, offering a few shout-outs to their fans.

"Last but not least, and I tell you it was a tough decision folks. First place goes to the Aurbor Grove Inn, for the second year in a row, for their Christmas Wonderland."

Jackson leaped in the air, clapping and shouting. "Whoo!" He nodded his head at me. "Go on up there and accept it."

I pulled Jackson's hand and drug him along with me. The clunky, gold trophy was heavier than I expected. The mayor passed the microphone to Jackson, who handed it to me like a hot potato.

"Oh wow. I don't even know where to start."

Jackson nudged his head in encouragement, offering a reassuring smile.

"Uh, many of you know my brother Manny who runs the Aurbor Grove Inn. I'm accepting this award on his behalf. He would be proud. Manny loves Christmas, just like...just like our parents. I know they'd be proud too." As soon as the words left my mouth, a tingling sensation warmed me from head to toe — I missed and felt my parents' presence at the same time. My eyes brimmed with tears. I swallowed the sob clogging my throat, whirling to face Jackson. The pride and confidence sparkling in his eyes strengthened me.

"Thank you to Jackson Oliver for his help. This would

have been impossible without you," I said, raising his hand into the air. "Thank you all for this."

Cheers and claps erupted across the entire courtyard. Exiting the stage, the bittersweet crest of emotions left me unsteady. Jackson helped me walk down the stage steps, his hand landing in the middle of my back, anchoring me against him.

"That was a lot."

"Yeah, but you made it through," Jackson said.

Before we could fully relish in our win, people I hadn't seen in years approached me, offering hugs and well wishes for Manny. Family, classmates, friends of my parents, middle school teachers, and old neighbors all remarked on how I'd 'grown up.' Each encounter lifted my spirit, higher and higher. The anxiousness dissipated, replaced with a constant flow of peace.

To my surprise, there were no whispers. No prying questions about that night. Just open arms and love. Maybe everyone had forgiven me.

If only I could forgive myself.

"Looky here, looky here. I'd heard you were in town." Aunt Rosa Mae slapped my shoulder. "But somehow I've yet to see you live and in person. I had to come to the Jingle Bell Festival to see my beautiful niece I ain't seen in years."

"I'm so sorry! I should have stopped by. I know better."

"Oh, child, I'm just messing." She wrapped her arms around me tight, then held my face in her hands. "I'm so proud of you stepping in for your family like you're doing."

"Yes, ma'am."

"That's what my baby brother would have wanted. I know he is smiling down on us." She rubbed her thumb across my cheek.

"Stop by the café anytime." She nodded her head in

Jackson's direction. "You can't depend on this one to always deliver your cinnamon rolls."

"I will do that. I promise."

"I'm gonna hold you to it."

The energy throughout the entire area was electric and contagious. And for the first time in a long time, I had the symptoms of the Christmas spirit: a gleefulness I couldn't explain or contain.

"You hear that?" Jackson asked.

"What?" I stopped in my tracks.

He started dancing, moving his head from side to side. Once again, Darlene Love begged for her baby to come home for Christmas.

"I'm beginning to think this is our song. I only hear it when I'm out with you."

"You're not gonna sing this time though, right?"

"Nope"

"Good."

"Cause we're gonna dance."

"Hunh?"

Jackson drew me into his arms and swayed to the music. I hesitated but moved stiffly with him.

I looked all around us, embarrassment rising. "Nobody else is dancing."

"It's either dancing or singing," he grinned.

"Oh, that's an easy choice."

With that, I leaned in, resting my hands on his shoulders. He laid his cheek against the crown of my soft puffy coils. His rhythm was as off-beat as his out-of-tune voice. But I didn't mind being this close to Jackson. Not one bit.

* * *

AFTER LEAVING the Jingle Bell Festival, we stopped by the hospital. 'Nurse Betty' met us at the entrance, and I endured her shameless flirtations and annoying laugh.

She really wanted Jackson, and he danced around the edges, instead of directly giving her a sense of what he wanted. It was amusing to watch him wiggle out of her hints of wanting to hang out sometime.

"That woman really likes you," I said as we hopped on the elevator.

"Trina's a good woman. Not my type, though." He pressed the button, then smiled down at me. I tried to repress my own, but I couldn't. Yep, that's all it took to send me back to butterflies-in-my-stomach, heart-drawing, dreamy teenager.

Manny and Alexis cheered when they saw the trophy. My super-competitive brother hugged the gold statue to his chest, then kissed it several times.

"See, I told ya'll it was worth it."

I raised an eyebrow as I sat the trophy alongside Get Well cards, flowers, and balloons on his table. "You're telling me that's worth a leg?"

"You know what I mean."

Post-surgery, my brother looked good and was hopeful about coming home soon.

"Jackson, could you take me to get something to eat right quick? If I eat another meal from that cafeteria, I don't know what I'm gonna do. Baby Jefferson needs a burger."

"She's already milking this baby thing I see," I told Manny.

"Do ya'll want anything?" Jackson asked, helping Alexis put on her coat.

Manny waved. "I'm good."

"I'll have fries. No salt."

"Are you always hungry?"

"Hey, you asked."

"We'll be back soon."

Once the door shut behind them, I turned back to Manny. Fuzzy hair sprouted on his chin and bags formed under his eyes.

"I can't wait for you to get out of this hospital."

"Sis, I know we need to get back to business so you can do the same," he said, grabbing my hand.

"No, I'm fine."

"I should be out by Christmas. Maybe we can celebrate together at the house?"

"You don't give up do you?" I sighed.

"Nope."

I wanted to tell him that duty called, but I couldn't lie to Manny.

"I know we're different, but this is a tough time of year for me too. Ya'll probably think I'm crazy for going all out on the decorations, but that's what I remember mom and dad doing. Every year, we had something bigger and better on the lawn. Somehow, by continuing their traditions, it makes me feel closer to them. Like they're still here in a way."

"They loved Christmas," I said, nodding my head. "I think they were more excited than we were sometimes. You know how they couldn't wait for us to get up and open their gifts, so they'd wake us up?"

Manny ran his hand down his face, his shoulders shaking as he laughed.

"It's hard for me to look back and not miss them. Not think about how things would be different, if we hadn't been in that car. If I hadn't—"

"None of that was your fault," Manny said, peering at me. "You need to know that."

"You don't understand. That accident." I paused, biting my bottom lip as the wave of emotion swelled on the inside.

My voice cracked, each word a hushed whisper. "I didn't have any injuries. Not one fracture. But it broke me. On the inside."

"Sis." He gripped my hands. "Look at me."

I avoided eye contact because if I looked at him, he'd see the scared little girl I worked so hard to hide away. I wanted to be strong.

"I said look at me!"

My brother never used that serious, gruff tone. I glanced into his dark brown eyes, and he automatically smiled at me in that big brother way.

"I love you. You know that right?"

I sniffled, nodding my head slowly.

"Our parents loved you. *Loved you*. It didn't matter what you did, what you thought you did, or any of that. I want you to see that, feel it, know it. They may not be here physically, but what we have — what we will always have is their love. They gave that to us."

His words seeped in slowly. I wiped away the wetness around my eyes with the back of my hands.

"The only thing that gets me through is to focus on what we have. Yes, we lost our parents and nothing could ever replace them. But, you know what else has happened? You found out you're going to finally be an Auntie! You're helping a couple get married tomorrow. You've made my best friend happy like I've never seen. You're helping keep our family's business going.

"We've lost a lot, Ebony, but we've gained so much too. When we live, I mean truly live, we pass on the very same love that our parents gave us. We create new memories to hold onto."

As Manny checked off the many things that occurred in this month alone, my heart swelled.

"And I want you around for many more. That's why I want you here with the family for Christmas. I want to make as many new memories with my sister while I have a chance."

To think, only a few days ago, I thought I'd never hear Manny's voice again, let alone be next to him. For so long, I'd taken so much for granted.

I took a deep breath, then slowly released it.

"Alright, alright, I'll stay through Christmas."

"That's what I'm talking about," Manny shouted.

"And I'm expecting an expensive gift too."

"Wait, hold up now."

I rose from the bed.

"No, seriously. I am not agreeing to that. C'mon, I broke my leg. And after paying for that surgery, I'm gonna be *broke broke*."

CHAPTER ELEVEN

I thought this would be me one day. I straightened out the snow-white wedding runner. Like an adult flower girl, I sprinkled pink petals of Christmas roses along the sides.

A bottle of champagne chilled in the ice-bucket next to two glasses and cupcakes I'd ordered from Aunt Rosa Mae's cafe. I formed a heart with petals around the display.

None of it was part of Elle and Jared's original wedding day plans. Nor was the bouquet of fresh-cut flowers and hypericum berries held together with a pearled, satin bow. But I couldn't help myself.

Witnessing Elle and Jared vow to love each other forever brought those dreams I'd written about to life.

Think about that. Jackson's voice resounded in my mind as the newly married couple marveled at the decorations I'd thrown together at the last minute.

I couldn't stop thinking about it. About him. About my own event planning company and the offer letter missing my signature.

I didn't have time to revel in the successful ceremony because of an early check-in. Going through Alexis' checklist, I made sure everything was in order for the next guest.

The Tulip Room, loved for its private veranda overlooking the gardens, was spacious and had a mahogany writing desk that matched the four-post bed. A narrow oil painting of yellow tulips hung on the ocean blue wall above the flat screen TV.

If it hadn't been booked, I would have slept there.

When my mother and father first opened the Inn, they had to threaten me to keep me out of this room. I always enjoyed sitting outside, writing, reading, and looking at the blooming flowers in the garden.

I pulled out the profile on the guest: Chris Culpepper. She would be staying for five nights. A special note pointed out that she was in town for an author event.

I knew her name sounded familiar. A queen of romance, Chris Culpepper books always featured heroic gentlemen and swooning ladies. When I was younger, I loved those stories and dreamed of my own knight in shining armor. After a few real-life "romances" of my own, I realized how fictional those people and situations were.

Falling in (and out of) love, in my experience, had never been that easy and direct. It was more like navigating a maze, and I often got lost in the middle. By the time I found my way out, I was all too happy to never venture into the unknown again.

I still read Chris Culpepper fairytales from time to time, living vicariously through characters with perfect love and guaranteed happy endings. That's what we all want, right?

"Hello?" a raspy voice called up the stairs. "Is anybody here?"

"Hi, welcome to the Aurbor Grove Inn," I said, jogging

down the stairs. A tall woman with peach-toned skin, wire-rimmed glasses and short wispy, burgundy hair rolled her bag across the hardwood floor. "Are you Mrs. Culpepper?"

"Please, call me Chris," she said with a thick, Southern drawl.

Chris offered a plump hand adorned with rings on four fingers. She caught me staring at each of the dazzling jewels and assorted cuts of diamonds, rubies, gold, and silver.

"Keepsakes. One for every husband I loved. I may not have been able to keep the man, but these always bring back fond memories." She laughed until she started coughing.

"Ah, interesting."

"Honey, you don't know the half. Well, maybe you do. Have you read any of my books? The Sanderson Brothers Series?"

I had, but I was fine thinking the crazy exploits and compromising positions that took place between those pages were fake.

"I must have missed those," I said, rubbing the back of my neck. "Well, let me show you to your room. Do you need any help with your bags?"

"I got it. Thank you very much. Where's Manny and Alexis?" she asked, before moving up the stairs with me. "They always take good care of me. I've never seen you here before."

"Manny had an accident and is in the hospital."

"Oh my Lord, is he okay?" She pressed a palm against her double-breasted pea coat, her red lips forming a wide O.

"He had surgery and is recovering fine. I'm his sister, Ebony." With that introduction, she started up the steps. "I'm filling in for a few days. I actually work in consulting in Atlanta."

"That sounds nice," Chris said. She was a bit winded

when we reached the top stair. I opened the door of the Tulip room for her.

"Who are some of your clients?"

"I represent mostly private businesses and corporations. My biggest client is Thin Quick."

"Oh, I've heard of them! I tried their meal plan for a while."

"What did you think?"

"Have you ever heard of that show *Naked and Afraid?*"

I hesitated to answer because I didn't know where Chris was going with this. "Sure, I've seen the commercials."

"Well, honey, I was *hungry* and afraid...afraid of what I might say and do while hangry. You know, I get so agitated when I don't get enough sugar. All that calorie and step counting?" She blew through her lips. "I couldn't keep up with it all."

"I can see what you mean. Being on the Thin Quick meal and exercise plans require a big commitment," I said. "It's not for everybody."

"I don't think they're for real people."

Just like your love stories? I kept the thought to myself. Manny's comment about my lack of customer service skills reverberated in my mind as I squeezed out a friendly smile.

"I know I'm a fluffy girl, but I don't want to look like one of them Victoria's Secret matchsticks. It'd be nice to get back to my pre-40 weight, you know what I mean? Heck, I'd take the size I had when I was with my third husband."

How did one question lead to this in-depth conversation? I thought my job was to give Chris a key and show her to the room, not listen to her take jabs at my client.

"I'm going to let you settle in. Is there anything else I can get for you?"

Chris looked around the room, pulling off her coat. She draped it over the white down comforter.

"Darlin,' I know the drill. If I need you, I'll give you a shout."

CHAPTER TWELVE

*S*omebody was breaking into the Inn. My cell phone was dead, and I doubt Manny had any weapons. Alexis' book of everything didn't include a protocol for this.

I scurried into the bathroom, looking for something, anything sharp.

Another bump from downstairs echoed in the still of the night. I hastily grabbed the hair dryer.

Now, when I watched people do it in the movies, I yelled at the screen, but when I found myself slowly walking downstairs and asking if anyone was there, it seemed like the brightest thing to do.

I saw the glow of light emanating in the kitchen. Then burgundy spikes of hair.

"Chris?"

"Sweetheart, did I wake you? I had a craving for some hot chocolate?"

At 1 am? Yes, you did.

"Were you up doing your hair?" Chris asked, nodding at the hair dryer. "Or did you come downstairs to *blow* me away." The terrible joke made her laugh so hard, her stomach jiggled.

"Oh, no. I just—"

"Come join me then. Alexis always sits with me."

In my opinion, this was a crazy level of customer service. This guest ventured into the fridge and cabinets like they were her own. I sat at the kitchen table while Chris prepared my mug of cocoa.

"I'm having a bit of writer's block, I guess."

"What are you working on?"

"My first time staying here was about 10 years ago. I never got a chance to meet your parents, but I always felt their spirit here." I swiveled my head around, confused by what this had to do with her work in progress.

"Manny talks about them all the time, so all I have are his stories and my imagination. And a girl like me, I got one heck of an imagination," she said, sitting next to me.

"The best stories he's shared are about their deep love for each other and family. I thought I might write about that."

I drummed my fingers against the side of the hot mug. Mama and Daddy had some wonderful stories. In those early days, some of the strangest people stopped through our home. But my parents lived out their motto: our home is your home. So they adapted to the strange folk just like they did the normal. Then it dawned on me what Chris meant. Those were our, *my* stories.

"Wait, you're writing about my family?"

"In a way. It's not exactly about them, but my story features a couple who create a bed-and-breakfast and how they change the lives of those who cross its threshold."

"You can't do that."

"Why not?"

"Because." I stopped short because I couldn't think of a reason, but I couldn't deny how uncomfortable she made me feel. "It's not your story to tell. Besides, Mama and Daddy only got to run the Inn a couple years, so I don't see how there's much of a story."

"It's going to be about them, but really about the people. And how they reacted to losing them."

I paused, not wanting to go into the details of why my parents were no longer alive. It wasn't her business, and it surely wasn't something I wanted shared in a book.

What was a heartbreaking plot twist for her was the worst day of my life. My fingers fell to my chest, searching for my cross.

"I was in the car. I know what happened. Manny wasn't there. You weren't there."

"Like I said, it's *loosely* based on them. That's what I love about writing romance, you have to give the reader a happy ending."

"They didn't get a happy ending." My voice rose, and I could hear the *thump-thump* in my chest. I wanted to kick her out. Right here, right now. How dare she exploit my parents' memory to sell some books? "Most people don't get happy endings like your books. It's all fantasy. Just a lie to make readers feel good."

"No way, Jose, that's not true. Every story I have ever written was based on real people and real love," Chris said. She wrung her hands together. "I don't write lies. I write about love. Love that bonds. Love that heals. Love that sustains. Love that survives beyond the grave."

"Yeah, but real love is way more complicated than what you put in your books. It's never that simple."

"It can be. Human beings like to make stuff complicated – especially love," she said. "Happy endings happen every day in real life. Now it might not look like what you think it should, but they sure enough happen. If you're always lookin' for the worst, that's all you'll see. Manny shared with me the best, and that's the story I'm going to tell. That's the beauty of life, we get to *choose* which stories we want to tell ourselves and others.

"They loved this Inn and every person that stayed here. They loved Manny and you too. I want to honor them by sharing the best of their lives."

"So you're going to tell me what happened with my parents, now?" My arms folded across my chest, I gawked at Chris.

"I didn't mean to upset you," Chris said, taking a sip from her mug. "Manny gave me his permission and signed off on the paperwork. I thought you knew."

"He doesn't tell me everything, apparently," I muttered.

"Maybe he was looking out for your best interest. Losing loved ones, especially parents isn't something you just get over. People will tell you, 'oh, it gets better with time.' Can't say I agree with that much. Grief doesn't get better, it changes over time. But there is a difference between erasing the ones we've lost and mourning them, Ebony."

"You don't know anything about me. Stop talking about my family and me like you know us."

I pushed away from the table to distance myself from her. *Why would Manny do this?*

What made him tell her about me? About what I did? When it seemed like all was forgotten and forgiven, the thought of my biggest personal shame playing out on the pages of a Chris Culpepper book for everyone to see set me on fire.

"You're right. I don't." She twisted the rings on her hand.

The ones from her four husbands! If she knew so much about love, why couldn't she keep one of them?

"But I know the heavy burden of pain when I see it. Darlin', it's etched across your face and in the hunch of your shoulders.

"I've carried the weight of the past a few times myself. You feel God-awful at first, then you get used to it being there, lingering in the clouds of a sunny day. Let enough time go by and the next thing you know, you sorta begin to lean on it. Turn to it instead of anything else because it's all you know. People throw around phrases like 'leave the past in the past,' but we all know that's not easy. And if we're not careful, the past will snatch away every moment of the present if we let it."

Oddly enough her diagnosis made me feel seen. She stated things I thought but never spoke. I didn't want to run and hide, but gleam as much as I could from her. Much like my brother Manny, Chris was a love warrior, refusing to give up or give in. Her insistent stance brushed off on me.

I admired her attempt to help me, unsure of what to say next.

Chris turned the ring on her third finger, round and round, looking off toward the den. Her body was still with me, but her mind had gone someplace else. A smile settled on her lips.

"You've held strong long enough."

Then she did the strangest thing. She hugged me. My chest heaving up and down, skin on fire, that woman held onto me and rocked me like a baby.

Her embrace reminded me of something Mama used to say: *Sometimes, you've got to love the hell out of people.*

I wanted to shove her away, but the gesture squeezed my heart. Somehow it was easier to give in to this perfect stranger. Everything I'd stuffed down, came rushing out. It wasn't a howl, but a low, cleansing cry.

"You don't have to keep carrying it, you know?" she said, softly.

I crumpled when she gave me the permission I'd never dared to ask for.

CHAPTER THIRTEEN

I counted to ten. That's how long it took for a webpage to load on my laptop. *One webpage.* I don't know what kind of 'high-speed' internet Manny paid for, but this was more like 35 mph.

"Is it up yet?" Samantha asked.

"No, it's coming slowly but surely."

Paula said I couldn't email her, but she didn't say I couldn't check in with my teammate via phone.

Loophole! There's always one. I needed this one. I still felt Chris' arms wrapped around me. I didn't have the urge to kick her out anymore, but I couldn't help but feel like she was taking advantage of my vulnerabilities and my family. *Why would Manny allow her to do this?*

I was so upset, I couldn't call him or Alexis to do my usual early morning check-in. Instead of marching to the hospital out of anger, I busied myself with the only sure thing in my life: work.

Eventually, the full front page of the Thin Quick website appeared. The testimonies I'd selected rotated from one to the next. Below them was a flashy video promoting Lourdés as the host of the pop-up event in New York.

"These updates look good. Thank you so much for taking care of that."

"No worries. The rest of the team stepped up too."

"It seemed like so much needed to be done. Looking at the task list, we're on track or ahead of schedule on most items."

Before I'd logged onto my computer, I was anxious and sure everything was falling apart in my absence. To my surprise, the project moved along smoothly without me.

"Paula updated the staffing sheet, and the team was able to divide and conquer."

"That's good. Don't mention to her that I called you," I said, thinking about my boss' decree and the unsigned offer letter in the folder.

Despite the top title, pay, and prestige, I couldn't bring myself to sign it yet, no matter how much I stared at the salary. Not being able to plan events anymore would mean I'd miss the look of satisfaction on my clients' faces, the adrenaline rush, and goosebumps when everything came together like I'd envisioned it.

I'd lose out on the lingering pride and joy of pulling together special moments like Elle and Jared's ceremony.

"It's been a good experience for some of the junior associates." The chaos of children yelling and dogs barking interrupted Samantha. "Sorry about that."

"No, that's alright. Your kids sound like they're having a great holiday."

"They are climbing up the walls. I told them I was taking them to the beach soon."

"Christmas in the sun, huh? That sounds like fun." At first, I said it to be polite, but hearing all of the excitement in the background and in Samantha's voice made me feel a little jealous.

When was the last time I had fun? I could not recall a vacation, girls' night out, nothing. I barely could think of my last lunch break. Everything was a blur of work, work, and sleep.

"I hope your brother is getting better. Sounds like things are going well with you," Samantha said.

"What do you mean?"

"You don't sound so *grinchy*," she chuckled.

"Hmmph, I guess. Maybe you're rubbing off on me."

"I think it's the magic of home. I feel different when I'm here, surrounded by family and the people who've loved me since birth."

"Mommy, you said we were going to the beach! We put our sunscreen on." I heard a little girl say in the background.

"Oh, no honey," Samantha began. "These children have slathered on a whole bottle of lotion."

I cupped my hand over my mouth to hold back the laughter.

"Ebony, I have to go."

"Alrighty, enjoy the beach!"

After our call, I reviewed some of the notes I'd scribbled down. With Paula's email ban and Samantha and others taking charge, I didn't have much to do except hope and pray nothing fell through.

I called a cab to take me to the hospital. I needed to talk to my brother about Chris. As much as I appreciated her, I still didn't think it would be right for to tell our family's story.

* * *

I BOUNCED down the hospital hallway, the floor squeaking with every step. Rehearsing my speech in my head, I knew I could convince Manny to see things my way.

Her writing a book is exploitive, and what if she adds in details that disparage our parents' memories? She probably won't do that — at least not intentionally, but...

When I rounded the corner and walked into his room, it was empty. I called Alexis, and her phone went straight to voicemail.

Maybe she was at lunch in the cafeteria?

I double-checked I was on the right floor. As I headed to the nurse's station, my phone vibrated.

"I'm headed to pick you up."

"Jackson? I'm already at the hospital. What's going on? Where's Manny? I can't get in touch with Alexis."

"Trina just called me and said they had to move him to the ICU. Stay there. I'll be there in five minutes."

The nurse at the station confirmed what Jackson had heard and pointed me to the waiting room.

There were only a couple other people in the stark white room. A TV overhead played the latest news headlines. Alexis sat on a brown and green striped couch in a corner, a vacant look on her face.

I rushed over to her because she hadn't even noticed my presence.

"Alexis," I said, touching her shoulder. She jumped, looking up at me, her eyes red and puffy.

"Hey," she sniffled.

I sat down next to her, wrapping my arm around her shoulder.

"It's going to be alright," I said.

"I don't understand. Everything was going fine."

"What did the doctors say?"

Alexis shook her head as tears began to fall. "It all happened so fast. I noticed a rash, a handful of bumps. Didn't think nothing of it. Then he had a seizure. And I can't...everything is all jumbled up." She pressed her hand against her forehead. "They called it fat ebola or embolus or something. I've never heard of anything like that. It doesn't sound serious, but he won't wake up."

"Manny's in a coma?"

"I can't make sense of it. Is he going to die?"

I took a deep breath, attempting to process the bits of information she gave me. I don't even know where the strength, confidence...the faith came from. My voice steady and sure, I said, "No, he's not. He's going to be fine. I'm so sorry you had to go through this alone. I'm here with you now."

"He can't leave me. I can't raise a child by myself." Her hand fell to her stomach. "I don't want to do this, any of it, without him."

My sister shattered before my eyes, and I did my best to put her back together again. I held her close, prayed over her. I did all the things I wished someone had done for me years ago.

"What if he doesn't wake up? What if?" she chanted.

I pushed the same question to the back of my mind, wishing Jackson would hurry up.

CHAPTER FOURTEEN

*I*t's the waiting that gets you. Minutes slowly churned by, and when you watched others in the waiting room leave or move on, it made you think the worst.

Manny had developed a post-operation syndrome where his fracture bone caused the fatty tissue from the marrow to leak into his blood system at a toxic level. That led to seizures, problems with his lungs, and respiratory system. His routine surgery had turned into a rare, severe condition.

Now, I understood Alexis' initial concern. I promised to never doubt her when it came to my brother's health.

For us, the next 24-48 hours would be the most important. They showed us scans of Manny's brain and walked us through recommended remedies and the tests they would do to gauge his chance of recovery.

At hour 20, my leg bounced up and down from the Coke and coffee I'd chugged down to stay awake.

Jackson brought breakfast sandwiches, but I couldn't bring myself to take a bite.

"Mrs. Rosa Mae's going by the Inn to check on things,"

Jackson said, patting my knee. "And I can stay there tonight."

I'd forgotten entirely about my responsibilities as a host. The window of my world had become narrowly focused on one thing: keeping my brother alive.

To think, I'd come to the hospital with so much anger inside. Once again, my selfish emotions had taken me to a place of hate against my family.

I should have already learned my lesson.

Chris Culpepper could write 50 books on my family, and I'd agree if it meant I would have Manny.

For the past few hours, the television had served mostly as background noise, but when I saw a familiar face flash across the screen with a BREAKING NEWS banner, I turned up the volume.

"What is it?" Alexis asked. "Who is she?"

My mouth hung open at the allegations. "The spokesperson I hired for my client."

Stunned by the report of Lourdés Michele going on a drug-infused tirade LIVE on social media, I clamped my mouth shut. For the entire world to see, the girl who loved the camera smoked and cussed, threatening to beat up anybody that had anything negative to say about her.

"I gotta go."

"Wait, what?" Jackson said, jumping up with me.

"Crap, I didn't even bring my laptop." I pulled on my coat. "This is a disaster. I have to take care of this."

"Are you serious?"

I ignored his question, rushing out the waiting room. I didn't have time to wait on the elevator, I took the stairs.

"Are you really going to go back to work? Now?"

Jackson followed me all the way outside, matching my

brisk pace stride-for-stride. "If I have to. You don't understand."

The sun at his back, Jackson sighed, impatiently. He shifted from his left to right foot, the brown grass crunching underneath.

"Make me understand. That's your family back there," he said, puffs of white air come from his mouth. "You're gonna turn your back? For a job that you don't even care about?"

"I've been here before," I screamed, pointing at the hospital. "I can't go through this again. We're sitting in there like that's doing any good. It's not, okay?"

"Come here." Jackson tried to pull me into his arms, but I pushed him away. "Go! I don't need you trying to save me all the time."

I tapped Samantha's number on the phone and walked away from Jackson.

"I'm already on it," she said, without so much as a hello.

"What's the plan?"

"I reached out to the Thin Quick people to have them remove her from the website."

"Okay, we need to cancel her contract. I'm sure there's a clause in there to cover us," I said. I paced back and forth in front of the gazebo, the grass littered with cigarette butts. I reached for my cross, rubbing it between my fingers.

"I can't believe I let this happen. What was I thinking?"

"Ebony, you can't predict something like this. That's the risk that comes with celebrity spokespeople. The life they show the world isn't always real."

Think. Think. Think.

I don't think they're for real people. Chris' statement came to mind.

"You remember how you were saying Lourdés Michele was too perfect?"

"Yeah."

"What if we flipped it and focused on real health instead of the perfect body. Here's what we're going to do. You remember the testimonies we pushed out? We're gonna move the Thin Quick success stories to the forefront and center the campaign on real people. A real workout for real people. Something like that."

"I like. I'm going to take a stab at pulling together the first draft of Plan B. I've already sent out an SOS to the team, so they're on standby."

"Perfect. I'm going to give Paula a call and update her."

I was in my zone, and the only hint that Jackson was still there was the ring of his phone. He didn't hide his frustration with me, but he didn't leave either.

"It's Alexis," he said, holding up the face of his phone. "Do you wanna answer it? Or do you need to make your important business call first?"

I let out an exasperated groan. "What if he doesn't wake up, huh?"

"What if he does? Manny is a fighter. You've got to have faith in that."

"My mom and dad, both of them, were in *that* same hospital fighting for a whole week. None of our faith, waiting, prayers, none of it helped them. So, what's the point?"

Jackson didn't even try to answer that question. He was the main person at my side, hoping and praying.

"Do you really wanna know what went wrong? I should have been the one in that hospital. Not them."

"Don't say that."

"It's true. If I hadn't been arguing with them about *you*, my parents would still be alive today."

Confusion knitted his eyebrows together. Hearing this little detail for the first time, I could see the wheels turning in his mind.

"Yeah, that's what went wrong. My parents did *not* want us to get married. They thought we were too young. But me, being me, I thought I knew better. We fussed and fought the entire ride. I'd never in my life seen them so disappointed with me. I did everything right, but saying yes to you messed up my life.

"I remember, clear as day, I was sitting in the backseat, and my mother turned to me and said, 'One day, you'll see.' I yelled right back at her. In those few little seconds, I hated her for it. For trying to keep us apart. And then, BAM!

"You know, for a while, I believed my hate and anger is what killed her. It doesn't make any sense, but none of it did. That I could come out of that mangled car with just a bruise and scratch, I didn't understand why it happened to me. Why did *I* survive? There was no way I was going to marry you knowing it went against my parents' last wish. No way. I promised them and myself that I'd grant them that. It was the least I could do to-to...make up for what I did."

Jackson stared at me, the emotional energy between us raised the hairs on my arms.

"If I had known," he started, then dropped his head. "I hate that you had to carry this all by yourself for so long."

The burden lifted from my own shoulders and placed into his hands brought an expression of anguish on his face.

His voice was low and unsteady. "You know, after the accident, I thought maybe it was best to give you your space. But I've always felt guilty that I wasn't there for you like you needed me to be."

"I'm the one that moved away. I chose to isolate myself."

"I should have come after you."

He closed his eyes tightly and swallowed.

"What if it's different this time?" he asked. I wasn't sure if he was talking about Manny or us.

Jackson's phone rang out again, a persistent shrill tone carried by the whipping wind. He answered it and his eyes widened.

"Okay, we're coming back up."

Jackson held out an open hand.

I was scared. I knew grabbing his hand and following him back upstairs could mean I was losing everything.

We heard Alexis before we made it to Manny's room in the ICU.

"He opened his eyes! He opened his eyes! Oh, thank God!"

Happy tears gathering in the corners of her eyes, she leaped into Jackson's arms. Manny slowly blinked, then closed his eyes. He opened them again, following Alexis' celebratory voice.

The doctor stood awkwardly to the side, waiting for Alexis to settle down.

"What does this mean?" I slipped my hands in my back pockets.

"It's a good sign, but we'll see how he responds to a few more steps. It will help give us a better picture of what to expect."

"So, he's going to make it?" I asked, tentatively.

"We're working as hard as we can to make sure he pulls through."

"Thank you," Jackson said, shaking his hand.

CHAPTER FIFTEEN

hen I woke up on Christmas morning, I grinned, then stretched my arms to the ceiling. It didn't matter that I was in a hospital, and the crook in my neck was proof that there's no comfortable way to sleep in a chair for five nights in a row.

My brother was alive. Not only had he opened his eyes, but Manny progressed along the markers quicker than expected. He talked, responded to commands, and even laughed at a few of Jackson's corny jokes.

The doctor predicted that he would likely return to full health. He had a long recovery ahead, but I knew we'd get through it together.

A few text messages from family popped up, checking on Manny and sending Merry Christmas wishes.

I re-read the text message Paula sent last night after receiving my signed paperwork.

Paula: I accept YOUR offer. Have a Merry Christmas!

I glanced over at Manny, sleeping soundly. Alexis sipped

on coffee, watching "It's a Wonderful Life." We weren't a picture-perfect family surrounding a Christmas tree, but everything was just right.

"Ho, ho, ho," Jackson boomed, walking in with gifts in hand. He handed a few boxes to Alexis. "Open the top one first."

"Thank you, Jackson," she said. Tearing away the gold and green wrapping paper, she lifted the white box. The familiar smell wafted my way.

"Do you think Baby Jefferson will like cinnamon rolls?" he asked.

"Who cares? Mama Jefferson loves 'em."

We shared the whole box between the three of us.

"So you didn't have any problems at the Inn last night?" Alexis asked.

"Everybody was good. Chris checked out yesterday. And I can report that the newlyweds are off to a very happy marriage."

We all broke up with laughter.

"As they should be," Alexis said. "I guess you're gonna be planning a couple baby showers in the garden, Ebony."

"Ooh, a Fall event. I can see the color palette now."

She rolled her eyes, then hopped up to toss the empty box in the trash. While up, she returned to her husband's side, stroking his forehead. The love between those two was enviable.

Jackson leaned over to me. "I want to talk to you about something. Take a walk with me."

"Is it a scavenger hunt or something?" I asked, following him through the winding hallways outside.

"Nope. I wanted to get you to myself, that's all."

We stopped at the gazebo in the courtyard, the bright

Christmas lights flickering. Jackson grabbed both my hands, and I made a funny face.

"Stop being silly. I'm trying to have a serious moment."

"Okay, okay," I said.

"This week, if I've learned anything, I know that tomorrow is not promised. I can't keep putting off things I want to say or do, hoping the perfect time will come around. The only time I have is now."

"I feel the same way. That's why I signed the offer letter and—"

"I don't care if you stay here or Atlanta, I want to be with you," he said, his words crashing into each other. Excitement boiling over, he talked louder and faster with that certainty I needed so much. "We can make this work. We will make this work. I'm not letting you go this time."

"If you would have let me finish, I was going to say, I signed it after making a few changes. Since I will be working with other offices virtually, it doesn't matter if I'm in Atlanta...or Aurbor Grove."

"Hold up." He raised a hand to stop me. "Ms. I'm never-ever-*ever* living here is staying."

"I'm going to try it out. Maybe I'll help plan a few weddings at the Inn. I don't know. I'm going to go with the flow, see where things go," I said. "You sure you can handle me 24-7?"

"I think I can. I wrote a plan." Jackson dug into his pocket, then pulled out a piece of paper. I busted out laughing at the vision statement for our relationship and charts outlining date night protocol, and color-coded key milestones, month-by-month.

"I'll let you decide if the tissue is rolled under or over," he said.

After I finished reading, he handed me a small, black velvet bag.

"You've made a whole production out of this. And I feel extra bad because I didn't get you anything for Christmas."

"Well, if it makes you feel any better, this is a regift."

I frowned at him. "Really, dude?"

"Trust me."

I eyed him as I reached inside the bag, fingering the necklace. *Was it a family heirloom? It better not be a gift previously bought for another woman.*

Once unfurled, a ring dangled from the silver chain. A very familiar ring. A ring I proudly wore at one time. The one I'd given back to him when I thought we weren't meant to be together.

"You kept it?"

"It was for you. It was always for you."

"I don't know what to say." The glint of the sun hit the diamonds sparkling in my engagement ring.

Jackson moved closer, rubbing his hands up and down my arms. From afar, we probably looked like a couple who'd just vowed a lifetime to each other. The only thing left was the kiss. So I did it. I closed my eyes and press my lips against his. His touch was every bit as perfect as I remembered — even more. Reeling from the powerful adrenaline rush, I stumbled back.

As if one wasn't quite enough, he planted another searing kiss, holding my face in his hands.

"I've been wanting to do that for a long time," he said.

"As usual, you're moving too slow."

"Seriously, I don't want you to think I'm pushing for things to go back to how they used to be," he said. "It wasn't perfect then, and it won't be perfect now."

"I know. I don't have a checklist for any of this," I said, giggling.

Jackson hooked the necklace around my neck, the ring plopping right next to Mama's cross, atop my heart. It wasn't beating like crazy, and I didn't feel that heaviness. But it was full. Full of peace. Joy. Hope. Love.

He lowered his head until our foreheads touched.

"*Baby, please come home*," he sang the line from Darlene Love's Christmas song nearly pitch-perfect this time.

"Ah, you've been practicing."

"Mm-hmm," he hummed, his lips wandering across my cheek. "Merry Christmas."

"Merry Christmas to you too."

I meant it this time.

DISCUSSION GUIDE

1. Is Christmas your favorite holiday season? Why or why not?

2. Do you think people overlook or misunderstand those who struggle with loss during the holiday season?

3. Sometimes it can be hard to get in the "Christmas spirit." Have you ever faked your way through holiday cheer?

4. Ebony buries herself in work and builds the perfect life, yet rarely enjoys it. Are there instances in your life when you achieved something you thought would make you happier, but it didn't?

5. The burden of a "heavy heart" is seen throughout the story. Have you ever dealt with guilt or grief that made it difficult to live a full life?

6. Ebony mentions that Jackson is her 'what if' ex. Do you agree that everyone has a person they wonder what would have happened if things had worked out?

7. How important are the kind words from strangers and family alike? What role did they play in helping Ebony heal?

8. Do you believe Ebony made the right decision to accept a modified version of her dream job?

9. What did you think of Jackson 'waiting' so long to reunite with Ebony? Could you see yourself spending years in love with someone?

10. For all of her life, Ebony wanted to create the perfect plan, by the end, she claims she wants to go with the flow. Are you more of a planner or person who rolls with the punches?

THANK YOU

Thank you for reading *Happily Ever Christmas*. I enjoyed writing it and I hope Ebony, Jackson, and the whole crew brought a smile to your face. If you enjoyed this short story, please consider writing a review on Amazon, Goodreads, and telling your friends about it!

Sign up to get more stories, free chapters, sales announcements and more: http://eepurl.com/DS_S9

facebook.com/lakeshiapoolewrites

twitter.com/justlakeshia

instagram.com/lakeshiapoole

goodreads.com/lakeshiapoole

Made in the USA
Columbia, SC
18 October 2022